MARRIAGELESS

ESR

ESR

An imprint of The Individual Publishing

85 Rio Robles E, 1403, San Jose, California, US

www.individual.pub

First published in USA by The Individual Publishing in 2015

Copyright @ 2015 by ESR

Book Interior Design by Red Raven - www.redravenbookdesign.com

Book cover Design and Drawings - Concept and Ideas by ESR and
execution by Janrise.in

For information about special discounts for bulk purchases, please contact
The Individual Publishing sales at 1-650-421-3869 or

business@individual.pub

ISBN 978-0-9966710-2-6

"To the little friend"

ACKNOWLEDGEMENTS

Having learned, with curiosity, something of the different shades of life, I was struck by the idea of writing down what I had learned in the form of a book. Since it was I who had this idea, I would like to thank myself, as a pure gesture of respect to the concept of 'the individual', before I thank others.

My ideas have been formed by my experiences, and by all the people I have seen, met, heard or read about in my entire life so far. In this regard, I thank my **Dad** for cementing the foundation of being open and of questioning the status quo, which has helped me keep my ears and eyes open and accept notions based only on reason, rather than tradition.

Next is the lady I respect and trust the most. To me, these two words are applicable to only one person I have known: *Vaishnavi*. There are few personalities which are so impeccable that I can learn and draw inspiration from them but can't claim to be qualified enough to go any closer. I thank her for being the reference and the standard, which I can merely pursue to better myself, knowing that I will never be able to achieve it.

Sushmita has been my muse for this book, and I thank her for the time she has spent time with me. Writing is a painfully pleasurable act, and as a writer, I needed to endure the same pain that my lovely characters do. I thank her for making me experience that along with her.

Finally, I would like to thank *Deborah* and *Elizabeth* for editing my book to make it error-free.

TABLE OF CONTENTS

MARRIAGELESS

PROLOGUE

My name is Mr. Rational, and I know I am not someone you would like if you met me. That would not be your fault, though.

Likewise, it is not my fault that I don't see a good reason for many things that most people do these days. I just cannot appreciate the dumb things around me. This is my sixth glass of whisky, so I have the courage to say that I really don't respect my brothers. But really, no one should say something like that, and really, it does not matter what I think anyway.

I hope you have not started hating or judging me already.

What I think is less important than the questions I ask. That is what I do. I ask questions. I have always felt the need to write a book that includes the questions I have asked in my life and what I have learned in the form of answers, and to share it with you all, but realistically, I am not sure if it will ever happen. I am too old now, and I might be dead by the time I complete the book. I have always questioned searchingly and shared shamelessly with the world of my brothers, even though it only brought me disgrace. But, I felt if I wrote a book, it might bring insight to another thinker who must be sitting in the dark and teasing the candle light with his fingers, trying to learn, trying to misbecome society and be another Mr. Rational, while the rest of the brothers remain asleep. Yes, I am the one who asked The Question, and I am still trying to get an answer. I could not stop myself from asking it. I had to. Let us see if the case is ever opened, if it is, I don't want to miss it for anything. It's been a long and lonely journey. It's not the loneliness that tires me now, it's the impatient anger in me against what is obviously wrong. Even more irritating is the fact that everyone is capable of seeing the truth, or might be, but they don't want to admit it. The reason I am writing this is so you understand why I asked The Question, which evidence has shown you all think is a silly one. Nonetheless, I must ask it.

The Question is: Is the institution of marriage still relevant? By that I mean: Do we still need marriage? And in the absence of this institution, would one get more fulfillment and accomplishment from life?

At this time, I need to make two points.

First, I don't have a bad marriage. More importantly, I did not marry the wrong woman; instead, I got the right—the best!—woman, and brought her into the worst institution. I agree, it's totally my mistake, no doubt about that. All I can really do is reason, and I definitely know that's not the smartest thing to do these days. So, I ask The Question, which is not a result of my personal life; it's a bloody outcome of things I see around me every day.

Second—well, before I tell you the second point, you'll need to excuse me for a moment so I can quickly pour my ninth glass of whisky—and please forgive me that I cannot offer you any. Just imagine that writer and reader can both sip the best liquid in the world virtually, through the pages and words. Isn't it wonderful? (I always feel it's not my mind that jets out the sentences to be written, but only my intelligent fingers under the mighty power of whisky).

Getting back to my second point, I have learned that the institution of marriage gives a sense of fulfillment and accomplishment to a few people, and I totally understand that.

That said, my question about marriage is not for the individual; it is on a larger scale.

I don't see a purpose for this institution in the present day. It's as simple as that. It's an unnecessary and unintelligent piece of baggage from the past. You might not be able to understand everything that I am talking about now, but you will. It is just a matter of time. As you flip through the days of your life like the pages of a book, you will see what I am getting at, and you might need to come back to re-read this. Even if you don't, I am sure that if you just wait a few more years, you will remember me, because my questions will be even more relevant then.

I am looking at my fingers, and I am so bloody tired. I have argued, I have fought, I have screamed, and I have shouted at people in the marketplace for so many years, all alone, but now, as I write this, I see that I no longer have that in me. I don't have it in me to make you understand. Now, I feel so empty in the absence of my purpose that I am giving up. I am not giving up on the subject or The Question, but giving up on my life, I guess.

Shit, I need to drink more to feel better—to feel sane. The question is killing me now. Oh, my bottle is empty. All my bottles are empty. I don't think I can sustain myself until sunrise. In that case, let me just drain the last drops.

I called you brothers, thinking we both were on the same journey of pursuing a better humanity, but I now see you were never my brothers, you are all just some dead meat produced by the millions with just enough life in you to do what's prescribed, but never to think. Sorry, brothers, I thought I could write books and share a lot of stuff, but I was wrong. This cryptic piece of paper is all I have to give you. Oh well, I'm sure my unborn book would not have mattered to you. However, as one of my last actions, I applied to the courts to open a case to examine the institution of marriage. I am envious that you might be lucky enough to witness it if the case ever happens. But I doubt it will.

All life looks meaningless to me now. All my questions, answers, and reasons. They just did not matter and do not matter to you. You never cared, and now, I don't care either. You are here reading just for entertainment, and that's not even what I have to offer you. I am sorry. Just forget it, and let me simply strike through this piece of crap as well.

I am not blaming anyone. All I am saying is why marriage? I can't fight my brothers any more. I sinned because I questioned. Yes, I sinned, because I questioned.

MARRIAGELESS

1

THE BEGINNING

THE NAKED MAN, THE QUESTION, AND THE

ASSEMBLY

BASIC QUESTION

"I cannot forget his pain. This is the place he used to scream and ask, 'Oh, Mr. Marriage, why do we need you?'" said Mr. Philosopher to Mr. Truth.

Mr. Philosopher could still picture him. The man used to kneel in the center of the marketplace among the well-dressed population of men and women, shouting and raising his burdened, sun-burnt face to the sky, his eyes closing in pain and his arms flying into the air, while the sun mercilessly bathed his naked, wounded body with its heat.

"He definitely looked like a hero. Yes, a naked hero, screaming alone. The nude man was Mr. Rational," explained Mr. Philosopher to Mr. Truth. They were walking in the middle of the marketplace. Everyone was bustling from one side to the other, performing their daily duties. The marketplace was the busiest, most colorful place, where all work, trade, prayers, and sacrifices happened.

Mr. Philosopher was everyone's friend. He could always be found in the marketplace wearing crumpled, dirty white clothes, discussing or debating the merits and issues of human life. He loved conversation, and always asked people questions that started with "why."

Conversation was key to him. He had no need for food or drink; conversation sustained him. A good debate filled his stomach; hence, he was hungry most of the time, and eager in his pursuit to find a person with whom he could strike up a good conversation.

Mr. Truth was an intelligent person. His features reflected his intellectual capacity. He was fit, tall, and handsome, and wore smart clothes: a well-fitting pair of black trousers and a white, double cuff shirt. The clothes fit as if they were sewn onto his body. His hair was slightly disheveled, but that only added to the impression of sharpness and intelligence he gave off. His lips were his best feature. They were always eager to tell the truth. He had a long nose and extremely sharp eyes that could pierce through anyone and find the truth. He found strength in truth, and had never felt guilty or regretted anything in his life.

It was Mr. Truth who requested an appointment with Mr. Philosopher in the marketplace to enquire about Mr. Rational and get up to speed on what was happening. Mr. Truth had been preoccupied with some other truths related to the creation of the universe, as well as life in other universes, in recent times. But the consequences of Mr. Rational's questioning of Mr. Marriage had come to his attention.

"Why did he ask such a question about marriage? Tell me more about what he was like before that," Mr. Truth requested of Mr. Philosopher.

"Of all people, there was one man who was always found in any minority group. It was Mr. Rational, of course," said Mr. Philosopher. "He was unusually taller, stranger, and more intelligent than his brothers. He hardly ever smiled and always appeared to be deep in thought about everything in his life. He thought that every move and decision humans made were worth thinking about."

"Interesting; his likes and dislikes?" asked Mr. Truth.

"He loved nipping whisky."

"Whisky!" This surprised Mr. Truth.

"Yes," said Mr. Philosopher.

He explained how Mr. Rational loved the whisky's journey from the glass to where it danced on his tongue, its smooth ride into his throat, and how it finally settled down in his stomach, fuelling his blood and puncturing his liver. Mr. Rational always said he loved making love to whisky more than to any lady on any given day: such was his love for the spirit. It was rumored that no one had ever seen him without a glass of whisky; hence, the sight of him nipping his whisky was a complete image of him.

Mr. Truth and Mr. Philosopher strolled slowly through the marketplace, passing colorful shops. Every shop, at its entrance, bore a photo of God, smiling.

"Tell me more about Mr. Rational, apart from his romance with whisky," requested Mr. Truth.

"Even though he never smiled, he did not feel sad. Miraculously, since birth, he'd never felt the need to sleep either," said Mr. Philosopher.

Mr. Rational felt sleep was a half-dead state; sleeping would interrupt the world of colorful, continuously running thoughts that he lived in.

"How about friends—did he have any?" asked Mr. Truth, stroking his chin.

"He was only ever capable of making one friend," said Mr. Philosopher. He explained that Mr. Rational addressed all people as "brothers," but never meant it in the true sense; that was just his manner of speaking. But all of his "brothers" considered their families or communities complete without him.

Mr. Philosopher said, "His brothers felt he was unwise because he was more intelligent. They felt he was weak because of his absolute strength. They considered him a loser because he was the most successful person they knew, and they considered him sad because he could never be any happier. He did not love or hate his brothers. He certainly knew they existed on the same planet as he, but he was not certain if they ever really lived life.

"I remember that night," said Mr. Philosopher, dropping his eyelids.

"Which night? What happened?"

Mr. Philosopher explained how Mr. Rational had met him in the marketplace while shopping for cigars and whisky. Since Mr. Philosopher was his only friend, Mr. Rational insisted he come home with him that night to enjoy a few drinks.

"Both of us had our vices, and at times our vices served as our common bond," said Mr. Philosopher, reminiscing.

Mr. Rational's house held nothing that could be called finery. Every object in the house had a purpose. A study table, books, three whisky bottles, one glass, one chair, candles to read by, and a window that was always open. Mr. Rational thought the window served the purpose of conveying his thoughts to the outside world. He could never close the window; it made him feel like he was suffocating. One difference between his house and all others was that he did not have a photo of God. That was a big difference.

Mr. Philosopher continued, "We arrived at his house, and he told me that his wife and children were sleeping, so we went straight to his study. I dropped clumsily onto the floor, resting on one arm, drinking directly from the bottle, letting Mr. Rational sit in his usual place with his usual glass."

Looking down as he walked, Mr. Philosopher said, "I still remember his face in the candlelight, burning with questions and questions."

"What did you speak of with him that night? Anything unusual?" enquired Mr. Truth.

"No, we both spoke, as usual, about life and death. That's it. That's all that happened that night," said Mr. Philosopher. "But I saw something new in his eyes. I remember his face that night."

"What happened next?"

"I went to see him again the next day. I had a strange feeling," said Mr. Philosopher. "We were once again in Mr. Rational's study in the darkest hour, after his habitual family dinner and drinks. We were nipping 55-year-old Macallan whisky and smoking cigars, talking about our lives and eventual deaths. Suddenly, Mr. Rational blew out the candles and fell into deep thought. I waited.

Finally, Mr. Rational asked slowly, 'Do I need Mr. Marriage? Do we all need Mr. Marriage?' This was the first time he had asked this question, and from then on this question became his life's mission."

Mr. Marriage headed the institution of marriage in human society.

"Why did he ask that question? Did he tell you anything about his marriage? Was he not happy in his marriage? Was his wife not loyal to him?" Mr. Truth asked one question after the other, curious.

"His reasons were only known to him," said Mr. Philosopher. He explained that he was sure the question had not arisen because of Mr. Rational's personal life, but because of everyone's lives, and because of how marriage played a role in society at large.

Mr. Philosopher continued. "The question apparently fatigued Mr. Rational so much that for once, he did not want to be awake; he wanted to sleep. That night, after I left, he forced himself to sleep for the first time in his life. He slept soundly and had a dream, which he shared with me later.

"In the dream, Mr. Rational was sitting naked in the center of the marketplace at night. There was no one around. As he raised his head, he saw a person who had appeared out of nowhere, crawling from a distance. For a moment, he thought it was a ghost or a god. But he realized, as it approached, that it was his own naked body, punctured with wounds and bleeding from the mouth. This tired body, with his own low voice, whispered in his ear, 'When your proud, old acts no longer excite you, when the closed family chokes you with their love, when you are no longer sane, when society acts according to its traditions, you will see the arrival of a true person who will clear the clouds to uncover the philosophical meaning of life. I know you will be discarded and insulted by your gentle brothers, and you need to be strong in order to continue to be indifferent to them until you end your life.'

"Mr. Rational awoke suddenly from the dream," continued Mr. Philosopher.

"Immediately, he regretted his decision to sleep. Again, he asked himself, 'Do I need Mr. Marriage? Do any of us need Mr. Marriage?' He said this aloud to his wife, who he had been married to for many unpardonable years. Later, he asked the same question of his sleeping partners, who had always whispered in his ears that he should marry them. He asked his brothers, who claimed their success at marriage made them experts, and offered unsolicited suggestions. Everyone thought he was a fool to ask such a question.

"Had the question not been basic and obvious, the answer would have been apparent. Quite often, people will say that the simplest sounding questions have the most basic answers, but it is often difficult to receive a simple, clear answer when asking such questions."

Mr. Philosopher continued explaining to Mr. Truth that in the case of Mr. Rational's question, he was never given a satisfactory, rational answer. He got quite a few regressive answers such as: "God says we should be married." That answer reminded Mr. Rational of a totalitarian state leader dictating the behavior of all his subjects.

He was also told, "It is good for children." But Mr. Rational considered that marriage could be either a positive or negative influence on children. Not all parents and children were the same, as if they were objects of equal length and breadth. They could not be generalized in this way.

"Husbands become faithful since they are bound by a legal promise," was another answer he encountered. Mr. Rational thought a legal promise could exact penalties for transgressions, but could never make an individual voluntarily faithful. He believed a husband would only be truly faithful if he sincerely wished to be.

"Marriage is the foundation of society." On the contrary, Mr. Rational believed morals, ethics, and values were the foundation of a society, and that a society could exist just fine without the man-made institution of marriage.

Others said marriage "teaches integrity, commitment, and morality." Mr. Rational thought that was a stupid reason, since integrity, commitment, and morality should be individual values, rather than attributed to a collective institution like marriage.

"Marriage offers security," still others argued. Mr. Rational hated that answer, because he believed banks, not marriage, provided security. Moreover, he believed security should never be the pursuit of a free individual.

Finally, others decreed that marriage was "a blessing from God." Mr. Rational declared that he did not need blessings from someone who hides and speaks; he needed reasons.

"None of the quoted answers impress me either," said Mr. Truth, lighting Mr. Philosopher's cigar. "What happened to him next?"

Mr. Philosopher explained that over a period of time, the answers to Mr. Rational's simple question became so complex and irrelevant that he gave up his full-time profession and his family, and he began asking everyone he met the same question. He desperately wanted to learn the truth. But one thing he had learned from the various responses he'd gotten was that God was related to marriage in a big way.

"Marriage and God, really?" asked Mr. Truth.

"Yes."

"Mr. Rational traveled from colder places to warmer places, from places where people had no money to places where everyone was wealthy," said Mr. Philosopher. "He asked the question of saffron-painted beggars, junky-looking imams, and white-clothed priests. For years, he was naked, walking the world from one marketplace to another, asking the same question over and over again of everyone he met. Over a period of a few hundred years, everyone got to know the naked man and his famous question. No one had any respect for him, but everyone loved the sensation he gave them. People never tired of this naked man unceasingly asking such a puzzling question."

"He must have become quite popular around the world, then," said Mr. Truth.

"Yes. After a while, God started monitoring his popularity with the help of social media," said Mr. Philosopher.

God loved being popular, and He could not allow for any competition, particularly from a naked, intelligent, sympathetic man like Mr. Rational. Finally, after waiting a few years, God called one of His assistant angels, who looked like any other human. God demanded that the angel bring Mr. Rational before Him so He could understand the naked man's rationality.

"That was generous of God," said Mr. Truth, while Mr. Philosopher picked up a few stones from the ground and lazily started dropping them.

They were almost at the end of the marketplace. All the men and women had already started leaving.

"Hold on, you need to know what happened before you can appreciate God and his 'generosity,'" said Mr. Philosopher.

"Mr. Rational, having been given a formal audience with God, complained about the institution of marriage. He claimed marriage was an unnecessary institution people did not need anymore. He tried to justify his reasons, but God disliked him and did not pay much attention to the man's reasoning. Though I was told God looked on his nakedness with delight before he commanded his angels to throw Mr. Rational out of his palace," concluded Mr. Philosopher.

"But why? Why did He do that?" asked Mr. Truth.

"I don't know why he looked at him with delight, but as for the other question, it's simple: God and rationality can never go together. You know that," said Mr. Philosopher, emptying his hands, throwing all the stones on the ground.

"So, what happened to him after he was thrown out? Is that the end of his story?"

"No, it is not," said Mr. Philosopher.

He explained that a few hundred years later, Mr. Rational had become an old, sympathetic drunkard, but he still asked the same question, to which he'd never received a satisfactory answer. Mr. Rational had even appealed to Mr. Law in the courts many, many times, asking him to abolish marriage from society, without success.

Finally, God realized this might become a global issue. He took the responsibility for arranging an Assembly, where Mr. Marriage would be prosecuted in response to the naked man's appeal.

"Why did He accept the responsibility?" Mr. Truth was surprised. "After throwing Mr. Rational out of His palace in the first place?"

"God can only live when the majority of people believe in him, and he could see that Mr. Rational's question was becoming a global subject of discussion. God wanted to address it and take the credit before anyone else could, especially before Mr. Law decided to get involved. But deep down, even God was unwilling to question Mr. Marriage," said Mr. Philosopher.

"Oh, I get it. Now I know why I was invited by God to the Great Assembly," said Mr. Truth.

"Why?" asked Mr. Philosopher.

"To prosecute Mr. Marriage."

"That's good," said Mr. Philosopher, and did not ask any further questions.

"Getting back to Mr. Rational—he must have been happy the case was accepted. You both must have celebrated," said Mr. Truth.

"*I* celebrated, *we* did not."

"Why?"

"I ran to Mr. Rational's house, carrying the good news of God's agreement to host the Assembly and discuss the case. I also brought a bottle of Dalmore 62, a particularly good whisky of his liking. Upon arriving, I saw Mr. Rational slumped in his chair, his upper body comfortably resting on the table. I pushed him, thinking he was asleep, but the naked man was dead, with a whisky glass in one hand and a piece of paper in the other."

"I'm sorry to hear that. But what was written?" asked Mr. Truth.

"There was a lot written and crossed out, but at the bottom of the letter was written: *Why marriage? Can't fight my brothers*

17

any more. I sinned because I questioned. Yes, I sinned, because I questioned."

"I am sorry," said Mr. Truth.

"That's okay. I did not cry. Instead, I smiled, opened the bottle of Dalmore 62, and took a shot in the name of my friend. I kissed him and then left," said Mr. Philosopher.

Mr. Rational's body was buried in a vast open space far from the city center. Mr. Philosopher remembered his last words at the funeral. He said to himself he would not visit Mr. Rational's grave every week with flowers, but he would do it once. Just once.

"I walked away from his grave and went about my daily activities. Death is the most obvious part of any man's life, and yet it is often the most surprising," said Mr. Philosopher with his chin up, hiding the pain of losing his friend.

Mr. Philosopher decided to write a book entitled *MarriageLess*, which he planned to dedicate to Mr. Rational. He wanted to visit Mr. Rational's grave only when the book was completed.

Mr. Philosopher showed the incomplete book to Mr. Truth.

Mr. Truth opened the book and read:

When a so-called sin is what pleasures you, then you know that you are better than your brothers. Their incapacity is their common strength, and your ability is your weakness. You will never be able to protect your bleeding wounds from your brothers' poke, since they benefit from your pain without ever letting their consciences know. They are all proud because they were told how brave their brothers were. They are all beautiful because they were told how beautiful their brothers were. They are all happy because they were told what happiness meant to their brothers.

I don't know if you were brave, since you never saw any bravery

18

in your brothers. They will not tell you how brave you were, even after every possible victory. I don't know if you were beautiful, since your beauty can never be defined by your brothers. But I always saw your brothers ogling you, even though they promised themselves they'd never let you know how beautiful you were. One thing I know is that you were happy. This is why you celebrated your own life choices. You didn't smile like your brothers did, when they'd bury their heads in a vacuum and laugh. Instead, you lived and smiled without the need of your brothers.

In that crowd, you looked alone and blind. Everyone around you had their own lamps to light their way. You repeatedly felt no need to carry a lamp, even though you had invented lamps for them. They looked at you with sorrow, seeing your curious life. You never asked them to show you the path and you never needed their light. All you needed was for them to live, to make the common people know what was common and what was simple. The simplicity of the superior has not ceased; in fact, it never existed. It is the simplicity; it is the common good; it is equality, which regressively marches our lives from stars to dust, from light to dark.

"You are quite philosophical, Mr. Philosopher," said Mr. Truth, as he closed the book and returned it to him.

"Isn't that my name?" laughed Mr. Philosopher, proudly making shapes in the air out of his cigar smoke.

They continued to walk together out of the marketplace, talking about the case and how God had organized it in the form of a meeting in the Great Assembly.

THE ORGANIZER

The purpose of the Assembly was for people to gather and question this one institution, an institution that had prevailed for centuries and had existed since humans first walked the Earth. The Assembly was being personally organized by none other than dear God. Everyone else on Earth was busy and expensive. God was the only one without any known profession. He was the cheapest laborer, so He got the job of inviting everyone.

Mr. Truth and Mr. Philosopher realized that the Assembly proceedings were the reason all the men and women had left the marketplace.

"Must be a difficult job to invite all of them," remarked Mr. Truth. "How did He manage to do that?"

"God has a trademark to his calls," said Mr. Philosopher. He explained that God traveled on a flying, winged horse and spoke with people in the middle of the night when no one was around. He spoke to people in their dreams.

Mr. Philosopher said of God, "He never gets tired of speaking to everyone in person, since his best traits are blabbering and preaching. Everyone is well aware of this."

Mr. Philosopher added that most people were in a deep sleep when God arrived, and their initial reaction to His unexpected visit was to demand, "Who the hell is this?" before they realized it was the almighty God.

Mr. Philosopher went on to explain that God had a way of

convincing people to do what He wanted them to. "God sells his love and his message by making people feel he loves them all equally. He is the only unpaid, loyal servant to humans. Few people entertain the idea of asking him how he serves them. They are bored with the delusional and predictable ten rules of his book."

Like everyone, Mr. Philosopher had received the invitation to the Assembly. It read:

God Presents:

THE MARRIAGE ASSEMBLY

God Presents: The Marriage Assembly

Dear Sheep, Servants, and Saints,

We are celebrating the case of Marriage

with Great Popes, Saints, Truth, Past, Present, and Future

May 28, 2016, 12 AM

The New Home of God

Tickets will be released starting today.

For more information, please call 666 or refer to the website Godlovesyouallequally.com.

Admission is FREE.

Food and wine will be provided, free of charge.

Come join Me.

The two friends started walking towards the Great Assembly.

The wind was blowing hard. They could see the huge building from afar; there were no other buildings around, just the giant Assembly. It seemed as if the wind had been produced by the giant structure, blustering intensely to show the Assembly's strength in withstanding it.

"This whole thing must be an expensive affair; where did the money come from?" asked Mr. Truth, looking at the Assembly.

"God got funds from churches and temples," said Mr. Philosopher.

Many of these were richer than the world's wealthiest banks. God had hired a team and begun constructing an Assembly Hall far from the city center in the empty, vast space. He had not realized that the grave of Mr. Rational was nearby.

God had inspired the construction workers by shouting, "In the name of the Father, the son—not daughters—and the unknown ghost, I want you all to construct the biggest auditorium the world has ever seen. It should fit all seven billion people on Earth comfortably. It should have a gateway for each and every nation. This shall be the greatest construction project the human race has ever known. They shall remember it until the end of time!"

"That is indeed an inspiring speech," said Mr. Truth, and asked, "How many years did it take to construct the Great Assembly, and was it really worth the money and time?"

Mr. Philosopher answered that after about a hundred years of hard labor, construction of the Great Assembly was finally complete. It had the biggest auditorium and stage in the world, in the true superlative sense.

"It was definitely worth the money; it's a great work of

architecture," said Mr. Philosopher.

The Great Assembly was designed in the shape of a cruciform, with a defined axis. The main entrance faced east, the direction of the rising sun. Seating for billions was set up in the nave, which was the main body of the Great Assembly. The central tower of the Assembly ran up to the heavens; the architecture had a vertical emphasis unimaginable to the human eye. The facade had been carved by the best sculptors in the world, and the end result boasted large windows with beautifully ornate stonework.

Each and every person traveled from all the nations on Earth to the new auditorium, which had been named *The New Home of God*, though everyone just called it the Great Assembly. Huge billboards hung above the entrances, reading: *God invites you to His new abode. Welcome again.*

Mr. Philosopher and Mr. Truth looked at the Great Assembly closely, since the proceedings had not started yet.

They observed the gigantic marbleized walls and the wide windows with glass snakeshead designs that cast different colors of light within the immense nave. The walls featured millions of sculptures of human figures, so large that their height could only be known if one were able to fly into the air to reach their heads. The ceiling, so high and far away from the eye that one had to assume it was there, was held up by pillars completely wrapped in gold and silver wire, with gold leaves woven into the mesh. The hands of the monumental sculptures and the sprawling mesh stretched upwards as if to try and bring the sky down to Earth. The phrase *Equal Justice Under God* was written in gold along the wall at the front of the Assembly. There was church music playing constantly in the background, which contributed to the feeling of holiness.

THE H BOOK

All the people on Earth sat in the Assembly. However, while they all sat together, each person left an empty seat between him or herself and his or her neighbor.

The question of whether humans were stronger together or alone was something Mr. Philosopher thought about often.

Even though all of humanity was in attendance, the Assembly was so humongous that the total human population looked sparse in its giant confines.

Mr. Truth observed that men and women sat on different sides, and asked Mr. Philosopher, "Why do they sit separately? What's wrong?"

"That's what is written in the book."

"Which book?"

"*The H Book*, obviously," answered Mr. Philosopher.

The H Book was the world's best-selling book. It contained all the rules of human life, including how one should live and die. The beauty of the book was that it had rules for every human action.

Because there were so many people around, Mr. Philosopher whispered in Mr. Truth's ear, "It is publicized as a book authored by God, but no one knows the secret: God can neither read nor write. God is illiterate." He smiled.

"Then who wrote it?"

"Thousands of years ago, the book was written by the world's leading followers under God's guidance. People believe this book is their guide to life since it is said to be the word of God."

Mr. Philosopher explained that questioning, disagreeing with, debating, or even doubting the truth of *The H Book* was considered a sin, and no one did it. Such unconditional love and dedication to the book symbolized the end of reason and logic. Instead, people were forced to follow the script literally. Because it was human tendency to be unquestioning and obedient, people did not question the instructions in the book, especially since it had been written by God. *The H Book* made humans love God more. The fewer questions they asked, the more love and blessings they got from God.

GOD

God was tall, with long, silky white hair, blue eyes, and a long nose. He had the perfect mouth of an orator. His long white beard fell to His chest and blew in the wind. He was aging fast. God was always barefoot; He'd never worn anything on His feet. He always wore expensive white linens, but the crumpled look of the fabric made Him look poor and sympathetic; this helped the poor and needy to more easily identify with Him. It was rumored that God was actually devious-looking, but no one had seen Him closely enough to determine whether that was true. God's appearance was mysterious, and yet every human who looked at Him immediately saw a father figure. People said God had a magic white halo around Him, which caused every observer to see Him the way he or she wanted to.

"I wonder what God's qualifications are," said Mr. Truth to Mr. Philosopher.

"He is not educated at all, which is what qualifies him to be God for the deserving people," said Mr. Philosopher with a smile. "God claims that he has the power to cleanse human sins, and that he possesses the power and responsibility to balance society."

God walked slowly, dragging His naked feet and His old white cloak towards the podium. He raised His right hand and lifted His head. He waved blindly at the sea of people.

While God was trying to interact with the people, Mr. Philosopher said to Mr. Truth, "Not many people know he has difficulty seeing things clearly with his aged blue eyes. God is old and almost blind, but he is young in his expectations. He is an attention seeker, but more importantly, he loves to experience the cheering when all humans praise him."

Everyone in the auditorium clapped, whistled, and cheered for God, shouting, "We love You, God! You are awesome! We all love You!"

"They love Him so much," remarked Mr. Truth.

"I'm not sure," said Mr. Philosopher.

He explained that even though everyone cheered, deep inside, they all doubted whether God had actually ever done anything worthwhile for their benefit, other than patiently listening to them. They had questions, but they also had fears that kept them silent. They had never asked their questions. They cared about themselves, they cared about faith, and they cared about the beauty and purpose of life, but they were afraid of the truth.

The people used God as a punching bag when they were troubled, and God did a great job of listening patiently to them.

Lighting another cigar, Mr. Philosopher said, "This patient listening could be considered the only benefit humans receive from God. He is an unqualified universal psychiatrist to many, and because of this, people will act to please him."

MR. TRUTH

Mr. Philosopher was going to ask his friend another question, but it was time for Mr. Truth to take his place as the arbiter of the Assembly. Everyone else had already arrived.

Addressing the Great Assembly, God said, "Allow me to introduce Mr. Truth. He lives his life outside time and dimension. He lives in the past, present, and future. He had no birth and will have no death. People of the world, I give you Mr. Truth!"

Mr. Truth actually had no gender either, but God and society thought men were superior, and preferred that everyone without gender be addressed as "Mr." and spoken of with male pronouns.

The crowd cheered for God while Mr. Truth got onto the stage.

"Thank you for introducing me and for hosting this meeting," Mr. Truth said. "I will take it from here. I missed some of the events concerning Mr. Rational and the construction of the Great Assembly, but I have collected the information from Mr. Philosopher, who was really helpful. Thank you, Mr. Philosopher. Now, I have a request for You," said Mr. Truth to God.

"What is that?" asked God.

"Can you immediately change 'Equal justice under God' to 'Equal justice to all in the name of truth and reason,' please?" Mr. Truth requested.

"Sure, it shall be done," said God, though He looked as if He wondered whether He should really oblige this request.

Mr. Truth then addressed the Assembly. "I was in a different part of the universe, and God invited me to this meeting to act as moderator of the Assembly, along with my other friends here on the stage." He gestured to the witness box, where a few of his long-lost friends already sat, and smiled, turning back to the audience. "I am happy to see all the billions of people seated here."

None of the people cheered for Mr. Truth. The people could not praise anyone other than God.

"Tell them the purpose of the Assembly?" God suggested to Mr. Truth.

"Of course," Mr. Truth said. "The purpose of this Assembly is to prosecute Mr. Marriage and finally decide if people still need his institution. We want to determine if marriage is still relevant today."

Mr. Truth looked around the stage and decided he was satisfied with the arrangements. Mr. Present, Mr. Past, and Mr. Future, the rulers of their respective times, sat in the witness box, along with Child. Mr. Future and Child sat behind Mr. Past and Mr. Present on a raised bench in the judges' area behind bulletproof glass. It was important to protect Mr. Future and Child from any shootouts; indeed, they were the future. Mr. Man and Mrs. Woman also sat on the stage.

There was also a special box on stage called the True Box, which was the property of Mr. Truth. It was the darkest and truest box in the entire world, and Mr. Truth would encourage witnesses to use this box if he felt it was needed. The special power of the box was that even if one attempted to lie while in it, the box translated the lie and the truth came out. This box was not able to digest any false claims. It was torturous to one with the burden of lies, and it was pleasurable to one with the privilege of the truth. The True Box had no place in time; it could be used in the past, present, or future. All it needed was a call from Mr. Truth. He could run any case or statement through the box and it would respond truthfully. But the box had to be used very sparingly in order to retain its power.

The humans sat comfortably and lazily in the gallery, waiting for God to speak again.

"What about him? He looks cheap. What is his role in these proceedings?" God asked, pointing to Mr. Philosopher, who was standing just below and next to the stage.

"He is part of the entertainment arrangement. He is permitted to philosophize during the proceedings, using his abstract speeches and poems, in order to encourage the humans to think," said Mr. Truth.

Mr. Philosopher wrote in his book, *MarriageLess*:

Welcome to my book, welcome to my story.

I hope you are doing well, and I love your look.

I will make sure that this is not gory.

I have actors in this playbook; they all happily hang across a tree.

At times, I treat them with my shepherd's crook,

Before I decide to set them free.

MR. FUTURE

"May I introduce the judges and witnesses to the Great Assembly?" God asked Mr. Truth with a smile.

"That is unnecessary," said Mr. Truth courteously, taking charge of the proceedings. "I will take it from here."

Mr. Truth gestured to Mr. Future, the first judge, who stood up to be introduced to the crowd.

"Let me start with Mr. Future. He is curious, eager, and uncertain. He is more interested in the outcome of the case of Mr. Marriage than many other people, as he has to live with the results," said Mr. Truth, addressing the people.

Mr. Future was of average height, with rounded features. He had a big head, large eyes, and amazing night vision. His strange appearance was the result of human evolution.

"I know him pretty well. Yes, I do," God said suddenly.

Conversely, Mr. Future had never met God in his life.

Mr. Truth corrected God by telling the Assembly that the very uncertain nature of Mr. Future meant neither God nor anyone else could possibly know him. Anyone who claimed knowledge of a certain future was a liar.

Mr. Philosopher added, "Just as the beauty of the sun is to shine, the beauty of the future is its unknown and uncertain attributes. No one knows, not even God."

Mr. Truth concluded by saying that all claims connecting God and Mr. Future were in reality false, though they seemed true to those blinded by faith.

God did not look happy at being contradicted, but said nothing.

30

MR. PRESENT

Walking towards Mr. Present and raising his hands to the people in the Assembly, Mr. Truth said, "Next is Mr. Present."

Mr. Present was neither tall nor short, neither intelligent nor dumb, neither confident nor unsure.

Mr. Truth continued, "He is the most confused of our witnesses, but I am very impressed with the progress he has made during his rule, especially compared to that of Mr. Past."

Mr. Truth felt that Mr. Present was in an interesting phase of his life, a phase he often referred to as a midlife crisis. Mr. Truth also thought Mr. Present wanted to have more fun than what God offered, and believed he was gradually becoming more inclined toward reason, but there were a few establishments, such as religion and marriage, which stopped him from advancing in his pursuit of reason.

God was not happy with Mr. Present, because Mr. Present was neither loyal to God nor completely against Him. Mr. Present was trying to transform things during his rule, and God did not like change.

Still, God said nothing, and let Mr. Truth proceed with the introductions.

MR. PAST

As Mr. Past sat clumsily, Mr. Truth continued, "Next is Mr. Past. As you can see, he is a tall man: too tall to fit into any modern-day rooms or thinking. But he is still God's favorite."

He did not say more about Mr. Past than that.

The impression Mr. Truth had of Mr. Past was that he was too orthodox and conventional to be of use to contemporary reason. Mr. Past was the most obedient to God and followed every instruction and every word of God's book.

Mr. Past's life purpose was to enjoy the beauty of his relationship with God and, hence, every one of his acts was performed in the name of God, and also in the name of the Father. God loved Mr. Past the most. God had always thought he ruled the world best.

Mr. Past loved God so much that he had helped God establish Himself in society. There were critics who spoke of questionable incidents during Mr. Past's rule, such as the Inquisition and the Salem witch hunts. But in his authority as ruler, Mr. Past always said only one thing: "In the name of God and the Father, everything is justified. Everything."

The truth was that even those acts of death were simply the result of Mr. Past following God's instructions. The institution of religion had held great influence over Mr. Past's rule, and the same religion had established its greater influence on marriage as well.

Mr. Truth knew this was the kind of influence that could not be wiped away, even after hundreds of years of Mr. Present's rule. He could see Mr. Present struggling to keep Mr. Past's evil influence away from people during his rule, but one could still glimpse the deaths carried out in the name of religion and God during Mr. Present's reign.

"I doubt that everything you said of Mr. Present and Mr. Past is true; I like all the rulers the same," said God.

"You need not doubt, because I cannot tell anything other than the Truth," said Mr. Truth.

Clearly, Mr. Truth was trying to take charge of the proceedings and not let God control things at all.

MR. MAN

"Next is the witness Mr. Man," said Mr. Truth.

Mr. Truth explained to the crowd that Mr. Man knew he was the only one who had the power to create new humans and grow humanity, but God had taken credit for this as well.

God did not react to Mr. Truth's statements. He still smiled, looking at the people sitting in the gallery. He did not want to give importance to the statements against Him, but He could sense that both Mr. Truth and Mr. Philosopher disliked Him.

Mr. Man was the key to humanity. Along with Mrs. Woman, he represented seven billion humans. He was curious and intelligent. He had the gift of being able to adapt to change.

Interestingly, Mr. Man had a wound on the third finger of his left hand, which emitted a constant stream of blood. This wound was the outcome of a marriage ceremony. Mr. Man always lied and said he had incurred the wound in his childhood; he was not permitted to tell the truth about his injury. He could not say that marriage was pain. Hence, he always said pain was beautiful.

By nature of his birth, Mr. Man had a tool hidden below his belly. The tool was the most important attribute he possessed; it produced the precious gems that had the power to create a child.

Mr. Philosopher thought a lot about the relationship between Mr. Man and God, and he believed it to be the most fascinating story from the time life began. He thought God had been triumphant in making Mr. Man believe in Him and His book, which taught miracles over reason. But certainly Mr. Philosopher knew that Mr. Man had another important gift as a result of his birth, which was the chip hidden in his head.

The chip was made of diamonds and could never be broken. It was strong for a very specific reason. When this chip was enabled, Mr. Man could know the truth and use reason to understand his life and the world.

Mr. Philosopher added to his book: *The belief is that when Mr. Man thinks independently for himself, a war will break out between Mr. Man and God. But so far, Mr. Man remains dumb, and God is safe. God knows very well that people with independent reasoning abilities do not need him. Unfortunately, the majority of humankind still does not use reason, and hence, God is safe in the esteem of dumb people.*

MRS. WOMAN

Mr. Truth walked towards Mrs. Woman and kissed her hands. She smiled at Mr. Truth, who said, "Next is Mrs. Woman. She is my favorite witness, because she is the strongest. Throughout time, the weakness of Mr. Man has been Mrs. Woman, though he has never admitted it."

Mrs. Woman was the most beautiful form of life on Earth. Her beauty came from the voluptuous and shapely nature of her body. Traditionally, Mr. Man could never see beyond her beauty, but her true value was not her physical beauty; it was her emotional strength.

Mrs. Woman also had a diamond chip in her head, similar to that of Mr. Man. She also had the ability to reason, but unlike Mr. Man, she did not possess a tool below her belly. Instead, she had a beautiful vacuum, and Mr. Man could not withstand the strength of the vacuum. He always gave his precious tool to her.

Mr. Truth had always sympathized with Mrs. Woman, since he believed she had been exploited, in the name of God, throughout history. He thought nearly all of that exploitation had been unethical, and had resulted in guffawing at the painful sight of her naked suffering.

It was rumored that God had brutally raped Mrs. Woman multiple times. The books and poetry written to describe her pain were very popular among men.

Mr. Truth believed that Mrs. Woman was not only stronger than the rest of humanity, but also all the gods.

Mr. Philosopher wrote about Mrs. Woman in his book while she was being introduced: *Mr. Man completes himself with the help of Mrs. Woman, but the reverse is not true. Mrs. Woman is an independent being. She sometimes dedicates herself to the strength of a man who knows she is brighter than all of his earthly suns. But a woman should always light multiple homes, for she is too colorful to be depicted in only black and white. She deserves her freedom, but instead, she has been chained to God and men for centuries.*

Mrs. Woman wore a gold chain around her neck like an animal. This chain was a result of the marriage ceremony she had been forced to endure. The chain represented the blessing that God had bestowed on Mrs. Woman's neck.

The men in the gallery thought Mr. Truth was exaggerating about Mrs. Woman, that he was partial to her and had not introduced Mr. Man with equal respect.

The women in the gallery were pleased to hear someone speak the truth about them for once.

CHILD

Mr. Truth walked towards Child, shook its hand firmly and said, "This is Child, our second judge, along with Mr. Future."

Child was small, and had a natural quality of movement to its hands and body that made it even more handsome. Its blue eyes were the most curious element on the Earth. It had the appetite to experience the world and gain knowledge, and fulfilling these desires would inevitable lead it to sin along the way.

Mr. Truth explained to the crowd that Child's beauty was not found in its physical strength or its appearance but, rather, in making Mrs. Woman feel like God, since she created Child. He explained that the beauty of Child was found in its beginning as something as small as a bean with simple, clean thoughts, and its eventual growth into a large being with complex thoughts even God could not understand.

Child's objective in life was to become a God of its own. It would not speak much during the Assembly, because Mr. Man and Mrs. Woman had told it to listen more, but it would pass judgment on Mr. Marriage, along with Mr. Future, on the final day of the Assembly. At the end of the day, it would be for the Child of the future to decide the future.

INTRODUCING MR. MARRIAGE

The last, and most important, person to be introduced to the Assembly was Mr. Marriage.

"God, call upon Mr. Marriage, please," said Mr. Truth. "I am sure You know him pretty well."

"Mr. Marriage, it's time for you show your face and face the Assembly," God called out loudly and vehemently. God did not seem pleased that He had to call Mr. Marriage forth onto the stage, as He liked Mr. Marriage a great deal and did not want to expose him to harm.

When seen from afar, Mr. Marriage was handsome, and had a permanent smile on his lips. But when one viewed him from close up, he was a much uglier creature, with white makeup, dark paint around his eyes, and long black hair that swayed while he walked. He wore a suit of all the colors of the rainbow. His robes were also colorful, and swung around his body as he moved. It seemed like he was using the appearance of his psychedelic clothes to try and hide the truth about marriage.

Mr. Truth observed Mr. Marriage closely. He watched every inch of the artificial smile as Mr. Marriage stepped towards the stage. Mr. Truth looked into Mr. Marriage's eyes with his sharp ray of sight, as if he were going to rip apart the mask of marriage.

The people were surprised to see Mr. Marriage walking in chains, with seriously tight security escorting him.

Surprisingly, even though Mr. Marriage had been born in the womb of Mr. Past, Mr. Past no longer liked him.

Mr. Past whispered to Mr. Truth, "He is no longer mine. I feel he has changed from a simple, clear-minded boy into this ugly, colorful monster. I believe that the ugly and colorful mask was painted by God. I love God dearly, but cannot hide this fact."

As Mr. Marriage was about to reach the stage, God cleared His throat and addressed the Assembly. "Today, we will commence the case to decide the future of Mr. Marriage. He has been a kind friend and, most importantly, a great gift to all humans."

Mr. Truth suddenly interrupted God, and said with contempt in his voice, "Here, I warn You not to influence anyone with Your sweet talk about him." Then he commanded Mr. Marriage, "You, walk faster and get onto the stage."

"This is the end of all the introductions," said Mr. Truth, looking at seven billion faces, rubbing his hands and getting ready for the prosecution to begin, while security removed Mr. Marriage's chains so he could join the stage.

Mr. Philosopher sang while writing in his book:

Do you like my friends? They are all good except God.

They have their own trends, but I bet God is most flawed.

They will dance and sing for you.

They will take chances and bring memories of what is true.

Sorry to say that I will have to end a few of my beautiful friends.

THE ARRANGEMENTS

Food and entertainment seemed to serve as the purpose of life for most humans from the beginning of time until the end of their lives. Mr. Man and Mrs. Woman, along with all the people in the gallery, soon got hungry and tired.

"It's already late in the evening. Go earn some food for your dinner," said Mr. Truth, releasing the humans from the Assembly.

Mr. Truth wanted people to go to the surrounding cities and buy themselves something to eat, but God did not like the idea of people working hard to get food.

"You give them something to eat," God commanded, looking at Mr. Truth.

"Where shall we get bread for all these people to eat?" Mr. Truth asked.

God looked out over the audience, and saw an old woman who had some food with her: a loaf of bread and a bottle of wine.

"Bring her to me," commanded God.

God looked up into the sky and broke the bread in half, then in half again. He clapped twice, and told the Assembly that He had caused a miracle: The food had been multiplied in a storeroom beside the stage. To everyone's surprise, when the door to the storeroom was opened, there were a lot of loaves of bread and bottles of wine inside.

The people were happy, and they applauded God. They applauded not only for this miracle, but out of gratitude for not working hard to get food. People love being lazy, and in particular, they love anything that allows them to remain lazy and to praise the Lord.

Amidst the celebration, Mr. Truth knew it was not a miracle God had performed, but rather, a trick. God had stocked food in advance and distributed it now, calling it a miracle.

Now that the question of feeding the people was solved, the next issue was entertainment. God had selected a group of women to sing and dance when the men needed a break. He never felt a need to consider what the women would find entertaining. The entertainers were supposed to be talented. They not only had singing necks and dancing legs, but they had also signed a few clauses that demanded they appear like tantalizing dolls. The clauses stipulated what they were supposed to wear and not wear, and whom they were supposed to seduce and not seduce. In short, their mission was to make the men feel as if they had everything they desired in their hands. The women had all signed these clauses and did their best to put on a good professional show.

All around the Assembly, screens were arranged so everyone could watch the entertainment. The screens were so gigantic that even a mere inch of a dancer's cleavage looked thicker than the stream of the widest waterfall.

"In mine era, tragedy 'twas most appealing to the mind and

soul, but anon, the aesthetic standard hath stooped to merely showing the rear," whined Mr. Past. "And, fie! Such buttocks matter more than the music."

"Things change, and you've got to acknowledge the change. That is the truth," said Mr. Truth. "There is no pressure to follow, but do not be blind and deny it. Truth, at times, is darker and uglier than a beautiful lie."

PROTECTION AND PROCEEDINGS

The Assembly had been beefed up with strong, dark, dangerous-looking men. They were all taller and more muscular than average. These men were the designated security personnel for the Assembly proceedings. They exhibited the important attribute of being dumb; they were too physically strong to be intelligent. Hence, they were excellent guards for all the humans, judges, and witnesses in the Assembly. They were dressed in black, skin-tight, round-necked T-shirts. They wore thick gold chains, black jeans, and belts glaring with diamonds that spelled out the word *COOL*. They also wore black sunglasses, even after the sun had set.

It was said that these men had used every muscle in their bodies to increase their size, but they were very frugal when it came to using their mental muscles. Their brains were never exercised. The men could lift a thousand pounds of iron with one hand, but they would never be able to add two single-digit numbers in a day's hours.

Other than lifting a thousand pounds of iron with one hand, they had other life objectives. One of their objectives was written on the backs of their leather jackets for all to see: *26" biceps, 58" chest. I live and die for these measurements.* In pursuit of these goals, the men exhibited strength and dedication. Humans felt confident with these men protecting them. A few of the successful security men would get the opportunity to join the Marriage Police.

Mr. Truth wanted to start the case by questioning Mr. Past, then follow him with Mr. Present and Mr. Future. During the proceedings, Mr. Truth would also be questioning Mr. Man, Mrs. Woman, and Child, along with Mr. Marriage. Since this was an open case, he encouraged everyone to raise questions or doubts while the trial was going on. Mr. Truth was open to the idea of new guests adding value to the trial. The idea was to get well-balanced information, and at the end, the judges would give their verdict.

Suddenly, the Assembly fell silent. With so many people in attendance, the silence in the auditorium was remarkable.

Mr. Philosopher told Mr. Truth, "It is nighttime, and humans sleep at night. Sleep is their custom and being half dead is their lifestyle. Humans don't know why they need to sleep in the dark and be awake when it's light; all they know is that it's written in the book that they should do so."

Realizing everyone was sleepy, Mr. Truth ended the day by saying, "Good night, everyone. We will start our proceedings tomorrow with Mr. Past."

Mr. Philosopher looked at Mr. Truth and smiled, because everyone was already deep in slumber by then.

MARRIAGELESS

2
PAST

HORROR, BLEEDING, AND TIME

The second day's proceedings began with dreary weather. The sky was drizzling blue rain, and a golden sun was playing hide and seek with dark clouds behind the dull brown mountains. The people in the Assembly looked tired and gray. On the stage, God looked glorious, Mr. Man looked sleepy, Mrs. Woman looked sad, Mr. Truth looked strong, and Mr. Past looked loyal, while Mr. Marriage continued to look proud.

God closed His eyes and lifted both hands in the air.

"In the name of the Father, shall we start the proceedings with a prayer?"

"No, please," said Mr. Truth. "We don't have time for that drama."

The people in the Assembly were surprised by his response.

God opened His eyes and said angrily, "Did you say 'drama'?"

"Yes, I did. If only prayers were capable of actually doing anything."

"Yes, they are capable," said God firmly. "You need to have faith, first of all. I still insist on prayer."

"I understand You, and I appreciate You organizing this event. But please don't try to control this. I will decide how the proceedings will happen," said Mr. Truth, turning his attention to Mr. Marriage.

God continued to pray, but alone in the corner.

AN OLD MAN

Mr. Truth enquired if Mr. Marriage was ready for the proceedings. Mr. Marriage was afraid he would be blamed for all of humanity's failings. He did not completely trust all the rulers of the different times, especially Mr. Past, so he begged for a volunteer who had seen his entire life to testify as a witness.

"I might have been wrong a few times in a few places, but I need a witness to prove I am not the only one responsible for all the sins of humanity," pleaded Mr. Marriage.

Mr. Truth accepted his request and asked those assembled in the gallery if there was anyone other than those already on the stage who could be such a witness.

An old man raised his hand, without expression. "Yes. I volunteer, but I am not human. My name is Old Man."

Old Man belonged to a cult called the AntiGodists. They worshipped the serpent that fell from the garden to Earth. Old Man had the blessing of the serpent, not God, so he had been alive a long time and seen it all. He was old, but proud and confident, unlike most humans. Though he was called Old Man, he had neither the wrinkles of an old man nor the look of a young man. He looked as if he had aged to a certain point, then stopped aging. He had been sitting on a stone for a long time.

Observing Old Man, God came forward and said, "Who are you? You look evil. It's better to avoid such people in the Holy Assembly."

Old Man looked into the eyes of God as if they had been enemies for a long time.

Old Man responded, "God and humans cannot avoid me; I am everywhere. My snakes roam the world in different colors and shapes. Sins cannot be left unknown to us, and we prevail without much notice."

Mr. Truth knew the strength of a person's intellect and credibility could be measured by looking in his or her mouth, so he commanded, "Open your mouth; I need to see who you are."

Old Man initially refused, but when Mr. Truth insisted, he agreed to go with Mr. Truth to one of the dark, deserted back rooms of the Great Assembly. Mr. Truth closed the door behind them.

As Old Man opened his mouth to show Mr. Truth his tongue, in that fraction of a second, the dark room became darker, and his tongue looked like a dark, shiny snake tucking itself back in. In the same moment, his face became like a boy's, and his hair appeared to be a heap of snakes.

"I know you," Mr. Truth said. "I know you are the opposite of God. I know you are the opposite of blind faith, the opposite of servitude, the opposite of falsehood. I trust you, and I will use you as a witness."

God was anxious, and ran to the small back room, clumsily holding His white robes, to speak with Mr. Truth and Old Man. By the time God reached them, both Old Man and Mr. Truth had just come out of the room. God asked Mr. Truth to get back to the stage, as He wanted to have a word with Old Man for a moment alone.

As Mr. Truth left them, God said to Old Man, "Since no one is around, let Me say this. I think, now, that I know you." God smiled, as if He had discovered something, and continued.

"You were supposed to be My brother, but turned into My enemy. There has always been a battle between you and Me. It's the battle between human truth and what I make people believe. Nevertheless, let us not get into the past. I am sure you must be tired after all these centuries. We both have seen the lives and times of humans. You have been trying to make them see the light, but don't you see that they prefer sleep and darkness? They don't want to be awakened," said God, while Old Man listened quietly without even considering a response.

God continued, "The way I control humans is very simple. The basic principle in human life is that when they get what they want, they don't need Me. Based on this, I have conditioned all humans to pursue what they don't have. I try to condition them in such a way that they need to trust Me and not question Me. They need to walk in the path of failure I set before them. You, on the other hand, try to make them successful; you are a very good humanitarian indeed."

God took a step forward and looked into Old Man's eyes.

Old Man just waited for God to finish.

"Listen to Me, Old Man, you little snake. You will never win. It will never happen, because I will always tease them. I do My best to keep them far away from any human success. I tease a man, for example, with a woman's body. I permit him to lick her and kiss her, but not to completely have her. I tease him with money and possibilities, but will never let him rest until he dies. When a human tries to achieve something, you help him. Shaping human achievement is the tantalizing element I offer. Truly, you help Me, My brother, by being My opposite. Otherwise, I would have lost interest in the human game."

God had to catch His breath after speaking for so long, then concluded, "You are indeed My brother, in the name of My Father—sorry, our Father. Say something now."

"I have nothing to say. Are you done now?" asked Old Man, because he knew that his cult had one weakness: they loved the human race. Old Man excused himself from God and returned to the Assembly to hear the testimony of Mr. Past.

A STRANGE AND HORRIFIC RUMOR

Mr. Past always dressed in an old-fashioned baggy coat with a white lace collar and a red cravat, black petticoat breeches, and a hanging pocket watch. His matching red silk stockings were protected by boothose that tucked into his low cut brown shoes. His hair was long, curly, and reached past his shoulders; it appeared to be a periwig but was his true hair. He had a thick mustache, and his hair was clean and tidy, as if he combed it continually throughout the day.

Mr. Truth requested that Mr. Past step out of the witness box and speak to the sleepy Assembly about the accused's status and actions during his rule. The rain outside stopped completely.

Mr. Past looked at the people and smiled. "Good morrow to you, sir, everyone. Prithee forgive me, as mine language is somewhat antiquat'd."

Mr. Past was about to begin his speech about the genesis of marriage, when he was suddenly rendered mute by a memory that crossed his mind. It was a dark story, which he had heard in the form of a rumor, about God in His garden.

Sensing this, Mr. Truth called Mr. Past to one corner of the stage and asked him privately what the trouble was.

Shaking his head, Mr. Past said, "Alas, I cannot telleth thee. Oft times, not believing the truth is more effective f'r maintaining balance amongst the commonwealth."

Old Man joined the private conversation on the stage. He looked at Mr. Past and asked, "Is it about the story that circulated as a rumor, spreading among several nameless but reliable sources at the beginning of the Earth?"

"Yes, it is."

"I know what he's talking about. It's controversial, and I understand why he is hesitating," said Old Man.

"What are you two talking about?" asked Mr. Truth, insisting, "We all need to know; one of you needs to tell the whole Assembly."

"We cannot! It's too controversial. Can we go to the back room again?" proposed Old Man, and started walking towards the room without even looking to see if Mr. Truth was following him.

Mr. Truth excused himself from the stage of the Assembly, beckoning to Mr. Past and Mr. Philosopher to follow him.

"You both are coming with me."

Looking at God, he added, "And You are definitely not."

Old Man sat in the dark room waiting for Mr. Truth.

Old Man requested that the others not interrupt with questions, and began his story.

"According to the rumors, God had a father, whom he called 'Father.' Father was a good old man with a barely visible appearance, save for His long, white beard, shining blue eyes, and golden crown. Father once famously said, 'One cannot see Me and live after that.' As a result, no further description of Father was ever possible.

"Father had magical powers that enabled Him to create anything and everything He wished. He designed the whole world, including every living thing that crawls, creeps, flies, swims, slithers, and walks. Around the same time, Father also had a son. The boy's mother was unknown. Father had never married; indeed, He never believed that a woman, a wife, or marriage was necessary in order to produce children.

"Father's son was named God. God was mischievous, narrow-minded, and unforgiving right from the start. God envied Father's dear friend and guardian, the serpent. God hated the serpent most when the serpent had rational discussions with Father, during which it would comfortably wind itself around Father's neck and rest beautifully on His shoulders. Because of this, God developed enmity towards intelligence, and hated the rational notion of questioning. Even in his teenage and young adult years, he remained steadfast in his narrow-minded and unforgiving attitude."

Old Man looked at the others and saw that they were still listening attentively. He continued, "Lucky are human children, who are able to successfully outgrow childishness! God did not have such a luxury. Father tried to educate God and corrected him a great deal. Father would say, 'You cannot be jealous, God, you cannot be childish; you need to grow up.' But God didn't change.

"God struggled with his adolescent instincts during his teenage years. By then, he was already bored with his father's garden and its animals and birds. He had tasted all of the fruits and all of the different meats, but he was still hungry for something he'd never tasted. Luckily for him, at that time, Father created Woman. He gifted Woman to God, saying, 'Dear son, this is for your amusement. She is all yours. She shall obey you.' God responded, 'Indeed, Father, I see her as the flesh of my flesh. Thank you.'

"God liked Woman, and used to play all day and night with her. One strange night, which was even darker than the darkest nights, God wished to blindfold Woman and play with her body. God said to her, 'In the name of the Father, I would like to play with you and your beauty,' holding a black cloth to blind her.

"Woman said, 'In the name of the Father we share, I am Your sister and friend, not Your meat. Promise me, in the name of our Father, that You shall never propose this to me again. If You repeat this behavior, I shall let Father know.'

"God screamed, 'I am the son of your creator, and in the name of My Father, you are supposed to obey Me without questioning. I am not your brother or your friend. I cannot have sisters, since Woman is inferior, and a female friend is no more than a humble meat to be served up and consumed.'"

Mr. Past was looking more and more anxious as the story went on. Mr. Truth and Mr. Philosopher simply listened as Old Man continued.

"God's angry shouts echoed throughout the whole garden while Woman wept and finally said, 'If You say so. I agree, in the name of the same Father. I am Yours and this flesh is Yours. Savor it, for I can't fight any more; I am now Your humble servant.'

"While Woman wept, God dragged her naked body under a tree, smiling radiantly all the while. The tree God chose happened to be the Wisdom Tree, where Father's friendly serpent lived and watched what went on around it.

"First, God checked Woman's chest and below her belly with his godly and unfriendly fingers. Then he threw himself on her, and began feeding as if he had been hungry all his life. God had sharp canines, which hurt Woman's neck. She screamed and moaned. He paid no attention. God almost broke Woman's back. He unleashed himself and filled her to satisfy the animal within him. Not satiated with the heinous act, God blinded Woman, and then sodomized her until she bled.

"The faithful old serpent was watching, and it pleaded, 'Holy Son of the Father, my brother, please stop this! Please stop this crime! I beg of You, in the name of the Father!' It slithered down the tree and wrapped itself around God's shoulders.

"God threw the serpent against the tree, and the wise serpent wept for the helpless Woman.

"God, who was prescient enough to know what Father would do to him, hurriedly threw Woman to Earth, which had been created by Father a few days prior.

"After a while, it became clear that Woman was pregnant, and the first Man was born. Amused at the idea of a Man and a Woman as his playthings, God thought up a human establishment called 'marriage,' which would work against their natural instincts and result in an entertaining struggle. He didn't create marriage, but the thought of it pleased him.

"The serpent, after witnessing God's crime, traveled immediately to Earth. From that day forward, it became a friendly companion to Woman and Man. The serpent displayed more loyalty to humanity that it had ever shown God, though this is a fact that people only dare to whisper late at night."

Mr. Truth opened his mouth to speak, but Old Man continued. "There is even more to the story. Some people believe that God killed Father a few years later, since Father's protective serpent was no longer around, and God wanted his secrets to remain secret."

"Why would God kill His father?" asked Mr. Truth.

"That is a story for some other time," said Old Man.

Mr. Truth took Mr. Past by the shoulders and asked him, "Did you know this? Tell me, look at me, God is not here right now, you can tell me the truth."

"Forsooth, this tale disturbs me," said Mr. Past, "but its veracity hath not been confirmed, and thus 'tis possible 'tis nothing more than a figment."

Old Man was already walking towards the stage, but he turned back and responded to Mr. Past, "It isn't just a rumor, and you know that very well."

Mr. Philosopher wrote in his book:

Did God scare you? Isn't he still lovely and warm?

Say you still love him; it's just the norm.

Marriage and Past join the horror.

I wish we had one less evil actor.

In this story of Marriage, where falsehood never fails, and truth never wins,

Let us see how Past unveils, and how Man sins.

MR. PAST STARTS HIS SPEECH

The crowd was impatient by the time everyone returned to the stage. People were curious to know what was happening, as they could only see God standing on the stage while the others were in the back room.

Mr. Truth insisted that Mr. Past address the Assembly immediately, since they had already wasted enough time.

"I shalt, I shalt, I shalt," said Mr. Past, trying to recover from the memory of the horrific rumor. He began his speech with a strong statement: "Marriage hadst naught to do with love and affection during mine reign. 'Tis all bunkum and balderdash creat'd about two hundr'd fifty years ago by these two rogues," he said, pointing at God and Mr. Marriage.

Mr. Past was usually very obedient to God, but whenever that rumor about what He had done to Woman in the garden came to mind, Mr. Past became disobedient and angry for a while.

Mr. Philosopher, looking at Mr. Past, wrote in his book: *While anger gives one the strength to disobey, it never sustains one long enough to make a difference. It is a useless emotion with no real effect.*

Mr. Past, still invigorated by his anger—though he was not trying to upset God—walked towards Mr. Marriage, reached out, and tore open his rainbow robes, exposing Mr. Marriage's chest.

Then, looking at the crowd in the Assembly, Mr. Past shouted, "This is f'r ye! Behold this!"

He pointed at the two words tattooed on Mr. Marriage's chest: *LOVE* and *AFFECTION*.

The tattoos were still partially red and wet, obviously engraved there within the past few centuries.

Mr. Past raised his hand and pointed at the tattoos, proclaiming, "'Twas God who execut'd these colorful paintings of love and affection on his chest. Mr. Marriage was an earnest nobleman in mine era, whose integrity was nev'r bas'd on the tenuous and gimcrack notions of love and affection."

He laughed, and said, "As it so happens, in my era 'twas pondered as a disgrace to showeth love f'r a woman in public; in some circumstances, 'twas considered a criminal act. History standeth witness to this."

God walked towards Mr. Past. "Easy, My dear son, easy. Yes, I did the tattoos. But it was for the common good of society," He said, slowly rubbing Mr. Past's shoulders with His hands.

Mr. Past continued to speak, as if he couldn't hear God. Now that he had started talking, it was as if he couldn't stop.

In his long-winded manner, he explained to the Assembly how Mr. Marriage had been born almost four thousand years ago, and that his objectives had been different at different stages in the past. He said that initially, as a child, Mr. Marriage had been a protector of women, and that later his priorities shifted to the preservation of power amongst kings and the ruling class.

Mr. Past explained that, unlike its status as a rather personal contract under Mr. Present's rule, marriage had been more of a social affair in his day. Thus, Mr. Marriage had played a larger role in society during Mr. Past's time. Mr. Marriage had helped kings sustain their power, at times even going so far as to make kings and the ruling class sleep with their own daughters in order to produce legitimate heirs.

A quizzical expression crossed Mr. Past's face, and he said, "It dost sound heinous to modern ears, but it nev'r sound'd anything less than perfect in the old world. Times wast different; 'twas oft times sensible f'r a king to lay with his own daughter with an eye to siring a prince on her. By dint of Mr. Marriage."

The people who had been sitting sleepily in the Assembly were shocked awake.

MARRIAGE BLEEDS

Mr. Marriage looked at the faces of these innocent followers and began dancing up and down the aisles of the Assembly.

"Yes, I did it. Yes, I made it happen to make kings rule the land. Yes, I made him fuck his own daughter. I loved it. I made him fuck her from behind to produce a son from the front. Magic of back to front, front to back!"

Watching him, and listening to his singing, some of the men in the audience spat at him to show their contempt. They spat as if stinking spit could cleanse Mr. Marriage's sins. A few strong men broke through the lines of security, ran to Mr. Marriage, and kicked him in the nose. Then a mob ran over to him, stripped him naked, and hit him in the place that hurts a man the most.

Not satisfied with this punishment, the people tried to split open Mr. Marriage's mouth. Eight hands held and pulled his long hair, while six more hands shoved his mouth to rip it apart. Two more hands pressed on his eyes, as if they could burst like bubbles. The judges, witnesses, Mr. Truth, and God wanted to stop this, and tried to push the people away, but their efforts were futile.

The men gathered more strength, and screamed out loud together: "Mr. Marriage, you are dead! You will be in a hundred pieces in our hands!"

Mr. Marriage was close to being torn apart.

Just in time, Mr. Truth and the security guards pushed the men out of the way.

Mr. Truth shouted, "Please show some decency! We have not judged him yet, and you all have no right to do this to him. We need to know the absolute truth, the complete truth!"

"But," a strong man screamed, looking at Mr. Truth, "he says he made fathers sleep with their daughters. How on Earth can we tolerate this and listen to his case any further?"

"Patience, please. Justice will be served," responded Mr. Truth, pointing to the lines written across the top of the Assembly: *Equal justice to all in the name of truth and reason.*

Mr. Marriage, naked, bleeding, and beaten, his mouth shapeless and pouring blood, raised his right eyelid and looked at the men. He gathered the courage and energy to stand and smile at them. As he smiled, another young man raised his boot and kicked him hard in the right eye with the metal sole. As the boot connected, blood sprang from Mr. Marriage's head like a fountain, and he fell like a tree that had been chopped down.

"Oh, my good lord," he sighed as he collapsed.

God started weeping, thinking that Mr. Marriage was dead.

Mr. Philosopher said to the young man, "You did not kick him because you were emotionally disturbed by Mr. Marriage's confession. Rather, you did it because you had a chance to share the hypocritical heroism of the mob. This is not bravery."

Mr. Philosopher looked at the people in the Assembly, and he wrote in his book:

Generations have redefined cowardice as bravery; it's only opportunism that matters now. The world is changing, and the definition of good is changing. Look around you, and you will tell me that what was fair and good is no longer so. Success has nothing to do with right or wrong; it is all about getting what you desire. In this battle without rules, it is only the unknown who will win, since no one else knows his weakness. It is no longer a world of the strong and the righteous. It is a new world, a world of you and your ambition. There is nothing in between.

MARRIAGE OPENS UP

"Wait, you bastards," said Mr. Marriage in a quiet, dying voice. "I need to speak! I definitely need to speak; I am guilty, but not completely."

The crowd, hyped up with emotion, did not want to listen.

Mr. Philosopher wrote:

Everything is justifiable in the name of a mob, or in the name of the Father, or in the name of God, or in the name of faith, or in the name of any belief system. One can never underestimate the power and stupidity of the common man.

Mr. Marriage screeched out in pain, banging his head on the stage.

At this point, God did not want Mr. Marriage to speak, for He was afraid the situation might spiral even more out of control. He feared the men might cause additional damage.

"More than truth, order is important," said God, and requested of Mr. Truth, "In the name of the Father, please stop this."

"Order is important, agreed," said Mr. Truth. "But the truth, which is difficult to digest most of the time, is even more important—even if it is achieved at the cost of order. Life under order but without truth is worthless. Now, please let Mr. Marriage speak."

God raised His voice. "You are not understanding Me, and I cannot explain right now. It's complicated. But I ask you to stop this."

"No. We will hear Mr. Marriage speak."

Mr. Philosopher wrote:

You say that it's complicated, because it doesn't fit your order. But what is order and what is complication, if all you ever saw after your birth was complication? Then that complication is your order. And the order that you think is an order now will be complicated. It's all relative, order and disorder, love and hate, man and woman, here or there, fear or strength, good or bad, moral or excuse, master or slave, husband or wife, friend or enemy, together or separate.

Thanking Mr. Truth, Mr. Marriage looked into the eyes of God and Mr. Past.

"Are you two bastards ready to listen to the truth in front of Mr. Truth?"

"We art," said Mr. Past. "Prithee proceed. We two hast naught to fear."

"Of course, My dear child, please speak the truth," said God to Mr. Marriage.

Mr. Marriage wanted the Assembly to know two things: the

reality of his life in different times, and the reality of his life in different places.

Mr. Truth said that he was going to give Mr. Marriage a chance to tell the truth about his past, but with one condition: he was not to use profanity.

"I know, my language is fucking filthy," said Mr. Marriage. "I'll try not to use any fucking profanity while talking to you, because I do respect you. But I cannot promise that my tongue will have the same courtesy and manners when it is speaking with others."

Mr. Truth asked Mr. Marriage to proceed.

MARRIAGE AND TIME

"Yes, I have changed over time. I have changed to accommodate these people, these bastards," Mr. Marriage said, looking at the people in the gallery. "You bastards don't deserve to hate me. The fact is that you made me evolve into what you see now."

He confessed that sadly, he had never had a golden era in his entire life. There had always been a lot of drama, and he had always been fickle.

"I have always been in a fucked up state with the mistakes, alliances, and friendships I've made in my life," confessed Mr. Marriage.

In a human society, when an institution becomes corrupt, it has been infested by the majority of the people in a society; the reverse cannot be true, wrote Mr. Philosopher.

Meanwhile, Mr. Marriage explained that his past was divided into different stages.

Stage One:

MEAT MATTERS AND SEX SELLS

"There was a time before I was born, before men and women dressed in the fucking burdened avatars of 'husband' and 'wife,' when men and women needed to be together in order to survive," began Mr. Marriage.

"They didn't think about any other stupid bullshit except survival. Man was physically strong and able to hunt for meat, while Woman was physically beautiful and possessed the skills to take care of a shelter and comfort Man. Woman chose Man based on the strength of his muscles, since those muscles meant security and safety for her and her children. In return for protection and food, Woman offered her sexy, voluptuous body to Man. It was common for Woman to say, 'Hey, Man, feed me some animal meat, and you can feed on my meat—but gently, please.'"

Mr. Marriage explained that in those days, Woman had the freedom to choose any Man with whom to have sex. "Man's life was simple and peaceful, like any other animal's. Life started becoming fucking complicated as the animal in Man was gradually tamed, and civilizations based on intelligence refused to admit to being fucking animals."

Then he talked about his own birth a few centuries later. As humans became more civilized, Mr. Marriage was born with the purpose of saving humanity. As a child, he was a protector of mothers, and women in general. To make women safe and free, he tried to educate men and make them understand that just providing women with meat, muscle, and sex was not sufficient. He wanted Man to marry Woman and stay together as a strong family.

"I was fucking relevant! I helped both Man and Woman survive together," said Mr. Marriage proudly. He continued, "Woman was treated well. There were no bullshit restrictions on her sexual activity. Non-marital sex was as normal as the sun rising in the east!"

He concluded by saying, "It was a fucking open world."

Stage Two:

POWER PROGRESSED AND
MONEY MATTERED MORE

"You started your life with good intentions; what happened in the next stage?" asked Mr. Truth, writing some notes in his file.

"I messed it up. It was all because of fucking power and wealth," said Mr. Marriage.

He explained that he had started to become painful to human society, because he ensured that Man and Woman were not able to live the way they naturally wanted to. He added further that when money entered the picture, his existence became all about strategic alliances, and the people who got married never had any say in it. The objective was no longer to ensure Woman's protection and freedom in the relationship, but to gain more wealth and power for Man.

"I was no longer a cute kid, but a fucking serious young man, dealing with relationships that were driven by economic motivations," said Mr. Marriage.

He continued, "Mr. Past ensured that the rich became richer. The equation was simple; Mr. Past and I conspired to ensure that Man and Woman married into similar economically powerful families. Love was never a good reason for marriage."

"Then what was a good reason?" asked Mr. Truth.

Without answering the question, Mr. Marriage explained, "Marriage was a fucking business deal. Marrying cousins or other family members to ensure that wealth did not leave the family was common."

Moving along, Mr. Marriage talked about polygamy.

"I was smart enough to allow rich men to have more women, and vice versa."

"Okay, was it all polygamous at this stage, unlike the present age?" asked Mr. Truth.

"Yes," said Mr. Marriage. "Monogamy might be the way things work in today's world, but polygamy was common back then."

"Really? I cannot imagine that. How about God, did He not protest against this?" asked Mr. Truth.

"Of course not," Mr. Marriage said. "It is clearly mentioned in God's favorite book, *The H Book*, with evidence of this tradition in many marriages. The book talks about the renowned fictional characters Avid and Olomon. They did not just have hundreds, but thousands of wives. People enviously called them 'two lucky bastards with lifelong sucky fuck fests,'" he said with a laugh. "God only changed things later, insisting on monogamy during the rule of Mr. Present."

"May I say something?" interrupted God, raising His hand to ask for a chance to speak.

"No, You are not opening Your mouth until I am done with him," said Mr. Truth, and confirmed, "If I need clarification about anything, I shall ask You. Thank You."

Mr. Marriage continued, "During Stage Two, Man married Woman, but it was casual, with no written contracts. I encouraged only nominal promises between them. There was no elaborate bullshit ceremony to mark the occasion, nor were complicated contracts written. More importantly, there were no vows for people to lie about in the name of the Father or God.

"Marriage was never considered an emotional contract; I was too strong for fucking emotional drama. I made sure that Man had to make love to his wife with the objective of producing a son. If Woman did not conceive, then Man would try to pursue another Woman with my help. As Man's purpose was protection of wealth and his family name in society, Woman's purpose was solely to beget sons. If she did not become pregnant, she was fucking useless."

"That is a sick thought. I need to say that," said Mr. Truth, sympathizing with Mrs. Woman. "Since God claims to have always acted for the common good of humanity, did He not interfere?" he added.

"No," said Mr. Marriage. "God did not interfere during this stage, since the men who dealt with me were wealthy, with a great deal of money and power. The poor could not afford my consulting services. And throughout history, God has been more appealing to the poor than to the wealthy."

Mr. Marriage continued, saying that he had had a flourishing business dealing with the rich and powerful. He had made a great many diplomatic and commercial ties, and his reach had become tremendous. He had personally known every human on the planet. He admitted that it was he who had established the Marriage Police, the law enforcement agency that monitored the marriage activities of society.

"You started your life with the objective of protecting Woman and establishing the family," said Mr. Truth. "Was there any of that older concept of marriage in Stage Two?"

"Of course not," said Mr. Marriage. "At that stage, I was no longer a protector of Woman. Instead, I allowed marriages to include beating Woman, raping Woman, and exchanging mothers or sisters for wives in the name of power and money."

Mrs. Woman stood and asked, with pain in her voice, "Why did you change so much? Why did you do that to us?"

"Money and power, why else?" said Mr. Marriage, winking.

"So, you accept your mistakes totally. Then where does God come into the picture?" asked Mr. Truth.

Stage Three:

MARRIAGE MADE A DEAL

Mr. Marriage ran his hand through his long hair, and with a little chuckle of disbelief, said, "God was bloody jealous of me. He wanted His share of glory, power, and control over human society. He met JC to make a fucking deal."

"Who is JC? Sounds familiar," Mr. Truth asked Old Man.

The people sitting in the gallery knew who JC was, and were surprised that he was being discussed in the trial.

Old Man explained that JC was a poor man who had gained in popularity because most humans were also poor, and could easily relate to him.

"Per his deal with God," Old Man elaborated, "JC's objective was to give God complete control over all humans. JC worked out a master plan. The first step was to establish institutions that followed God's agenda of complete power over human society. These institutions were called churches. The churches were tasked with getting into people's private lives. In order to get into their private lives, the best person to consult was Mr. Marriage, who not only had all the rich and influential people in his pocket, but also had the reach to connect all humans."

"Okay. Did JC meet with you?" Mr. Truth asked Mr. Marriage.

"Yes, I did meet with that bastard, and that was my mistake. Had I not, I would not be sitting in front of these fucked up people waiting to be judged right now."

"Will you please avoid profanity? I am not going to ask you again," said Mr. Truth.

"I cannot do it any more, then. Just fuck it!" screamed Mr. Marriage. "Let some other fucker tell you, in that case."

Mr. Truth sighed. "Please, just continue. I insist."

Mr. Marriage looked at Mrs. Woman. "If only she would suck my dick," he said, and started laughing hysterically in his usual style.

Mrs. Woman walked towards him, steadily looking into his eyes, and slapped him hard.

"Never again," said Mrs. Woman.

Mr. Marriage, who was already wounded and near death, fainted, his head hitting the stage with a loud sound.

"Please, get back to your seat," Mr. Truth instructed Mrs. Woman. "You are not supposed to lose your temper."

Since Mr. Marriage was unconscious, Mr. Truth asked Old Man to continue so as not to waste the Assembly's time.

Old Man went on with the story. "The poor JC came to consult with the wealthy and powerful Mr. Marriage. JC had written a business plan to make God's grand vision a reality. All humans were participants in His vision. He wanted to intrude into each and every human's house."

"I still don't understand who JC was," said Mr. Truth.

"It does not matter right now," said Old Man.

God was relieved that Old Man did not disclose any more. JC was one of the many sons God had as a result of raping women.

MARRIAGE JOINS GOD AND JC

"God and JC observed that Mr. Marriage was getting tired of managing finance and power," explained Old Man. "JC bribed Mr. Marriage and Mr. Past with a great deal of money and many beautiful prostitutes. Mr. Marriage could not refuse the best flesh and money, and JC was personally responsible for handpicking the beauties."

"What did they want from Mr. Marriage?"

"Control, what else?" said Old Man.

He explained that in the new coalition, Mr. Marriage agreed with God and JC that he would only accept men and women for marriage if they abided by the rules of the church. JC appointed God the head of the Marriage Police. He also wrote a speech for Mr. Marriage to make as a public announcement in the open markets of the world.

The speech went as follows: "Things change, and they change for the good. I hereby declare that henceforth all men and women require my endorsement for getting married and must go through the platform of the church. I have new friends, God and JC, and they will help make this experience easier and simpler for you."

"I still remember," said Old Man. "God and JC sat happily in a far corner and witnessed this monumental moment in history. They could foresee how people would become slaves to the church and God in the name of marriage. That was how God and JC infiltrated every human's house with the help of the church."

"Okay, anything else?" asked Mr. Truth.

"Yes, there's more," said Old Man.

He explained that JC had observed how not all people worshipped one God. People worshipped entities as diverse as meat, animals, wood, trees, rain, earth, fire, water, or sky, based on their need to find purpose and meaning in life. That sounded dangerously rational to JC. He and God then conspired to wipe out reason from society, since they both knew that the rational person does not need God. They clearly sensed that thinking people would be very harmful to their mission of human obedience to God.

"So, God demanded that JC make the church the only institution that could establish franchises for selling faith. Faith had to be blinded. 'Kill reason, in the name of the Father,' was God's command," concluded Old Man.

KILL REASON

"How did God kill reason?" asked Mr. Truth.

"He identified it, gathered it, and butchered it. How else?" replied Old Man. "And JC was the mastermind. First, JC recommended that they identify people who were intellectuals. To JC's pleasure, analysis had proven that the majority of people were lazy and unintelligent. They were vulnerable, and ready to give away what little they had. They were poor mostly because they were lazy, or they had never gotten an opportunity to think past their basic needs for food, clothing, and shelter."

"Where did they find all these unintelligent people?" asked Mr. Truth.

"That's a no-brainer," said Old Man.

He explained that identifying unintelligent people was easy, since they were often lying lazy and drunk in the streets, or begging, or walking around without purpose.

"There was another attribute that made lazy people special. They whined and complained about their lives and the world around them. But they never did anything to improve their lots," said Old Man, making a signification population of people in the gallery uncomfortable, since they could relate to being lazy and unintelligent.

Old Man continued, "So, in the process of collecting the brainless majority, the Marriage Police gathered beggars, petty thieves, and rapists, who were the true followers of God."

"What did God do to them?" asked Mr. Truth.

Old Man answered, "He made the poor powerful and the rich weaker. He made the poor and weak believe that they were equal to the rich and hardworking, that they were equal to the thinkers and the philosophers. God knew how to destroy rational people. He needed to kill reason and knowledge, not physical bodies.

"God and JC had directed the Marriage Police and the brainless mass of human followers to be destructive," Old Man elaborated. "They destroyed the libraries and the cultural traditions that upheld rationality in any way. It was all done in the name of making God the one that all people would worship. The people who were the most destructive were later nominated as saints. And during this process of destruction, people were so impressed with JC and his leadership that they began worshipping him as the son of God."

"That was sad, to destroy the intellectual assets of society," said Mr. Truth. "What happened to the intellectuals? Were they imprisoned?"

"Prison would have been heavenly compared to what happened to them," said Old Man. "The minority intellectuals were not just killed; they were raped and cut into many pieces. When the fanatical God-lovers had cut the intelligent men and women into many pieces, they were scared of their blood, for it held wisdom, and lovers of faith cannot digest logic. Wisdom scared them even more, and in that frightened state they pounded on the bodies hysterically. That bloody pounding made the rest of society fearful, and fear prevented them from fighting against their own stupidity and ignorance."

Even today, the very definition of the common rule of democracy has the basic principle of majority rules. Just the majority matters, nothing else, wrote Mr. Philosopher, and sang a song as he copied into the book:

Hello, you again, did you ever think that such Marriage existed?

Indeed, there were a few rational men whose blood had to flood

to make God's will into reality, but at a dear cost.

The cost of my life, and the cost of your freedom.

Keep reading; the worst of the past is yet to come.

Your reason will keep asking, but you will get no answers in the noise of God's anthem.

The past is aging, but there are more of God's devils to become.

Stage Four:

VOWS WOWED

"After killing most of the intellectuals, what was left? What was the next stage of the plan?" asked Mr. Truth.

"Obviously, to bring religion into play," said Old Man. "God became a close friend of Mr. Marriage. Mr. Marriage started calling the union between Man and Woman 'sacred' only if it was done in God's presence and within a church. This is when people started making vows.

"Initially, there were many people who married outside of the church, but they were all punished and unblessed. The unblessed were sent to Death Mountain by the Marriage Police. To be blessed, Man and Woman needed Mr. Marriage's approval in the presence of God. The new definition of marriage sounded holy, as God had the beauty of language to say, 'Marriage is an opportunity not only to love, but also to forgive, provided it happens in My presence.'"

Mr. Marriage was gaining consciousness on the stage.

"Stop fucking hitting me, you bitch," he shouted at Mrs. Woman, who had been seated and listening to Old Man's narrative.

"You drink some water and relax for a while," Mr. Truth told him. "I am getting information from Old Man."

COMPLAINTS ABOUT POLYGAMY

Mr. Truth repeated the question, "What happened to polygamy? Mr. Marriage said it was common then."

"God killed it," said Old Man. "As God started taking control of marriage, with the help of the church, attitudes toward polygamy changed."

"But why?" asked Mr. Truth.

"It started with one poor man's complaint about the rich and able," said Old Man. "According to reliable sources, this lazy man asked God, 'Why should the rich and hardworking have more wives, while no lady in this world wants to sleep with me? Is it because I am poor and lazy? But I am Your follower. I follow You better than the rich and the intelligent.'"

"What did God say?"

"Nothing, but Mr. Past did speak up. He said, 'Thee nev'r toil'd hard, so thee nev'r accrued coin, so thee nev'r becameth a real man, hence thee do not deserve to asketh more of ordinary life, including a lady to catch but a wink with.' In response, the poor man said, 'I am a loser, but losers are the majority.'"

Mr. Philosopher wrote in his book: *The weak prefer to rule even though they are not powerful; they prefer to stand even though they have weak legs. They prefer to lead even though they lack courage. They want women even though they cannot make them happy.*

The people in the gallery were looking around at each other uncomfortably. No one wanted to admit to being lazy and unintelligent. Most people wore expressions that tried to say, "I'm not one of the ignorant masses," but they all secretly feared they were.

"God was smart," Old Man continued. "He sensed the majority movement and realized that the rich and hardworking were only a handful of the people. He preferred to favor the poor."

"But the rich must be powerful. Did they agree with God, just based on one poor man's question?" asked Mr. Truth.

"No, not at the beginning," said Old Man.

He explained that after a few centuries, God no longer allowed the rich the privilege of having many wives.

"There was a war," Old Man said sadly, "which pitted God, Mr. Past, and Mr. Marriage against the kings and the nobles. Eventually, God won, with the help of his millions of armies of faith followers. At the end of the war, the church eventually prevailed and monogamy became central to the idea of marriage."

Mr. Philosopher wrote: *It's the nature of the world that the superiors are always dragged down by the inferiors to their level. The superiors are dragged down in the name of equality and justice. It is most unjust to equate superiors with inferiors, calling truth falsehood, calling strong weak, calling tall short. But the followers of God are always short, weak, false, lazy, and inferior.*

Old Man's story was still not done.

He continued, "The rich and hardworking men needed more than the poor and mediocre men. They needed more challenges, more luxuries, more pain, more gain, more women, and definitely more pleasure. They reached an agreement with God, Mr. Past, and Mr. Marriage that they would not marry more than one woman, but would engage in extramarital affairs."

"Did God and Mr. Marriage agree?" asked Mr. Truth.

"Of course," said Old Man. "God and Mr. Marriage agreed overwhelmingly with this plan, which included a promise of significant funding for the church. But they were biased towards men and against women. Women who stepped outside their marriages for the same pleasure faced serious risk of public death, while men were successful in finding pleasure in the darker corners of the world."

GOD SONGS

The people sitting in the gallery were absorbing a lot of information that they had never known before. They could believe everything that had been said against Mr. Marriage and JC, but they still could not believe anything against God.

"What happened next?" asked Mr. Truth.

"By then, God, JC, and Mr. Marriage had been mostly successful in ridding society of rationality," said Old Man.

"Men started smiling more and women started acting more. Men who had a conscience, or any moral code, were punished. Dumbness beat out rationality, and there were many banners around the world that proclaimed: *We are all dumb! We love it, and we love You, God!*"

"Insane," remarked Mr. Truth.

"That's not all," said Old Man. "God and Mr. Marriage wanted to control even more. They wanted not only to stop people from thinking, but to strip them of any leftover freedom and make them completely dependent, as a free person can be a dangerous commodity among weak God-lovers. God wanted to test people to determine how dumb they truly were. God knew that people loved amusement, as was evident in every part of their lives. In the name of this very amusement, Mr. Marriage wrote a few poems a few hundred years back that have become popular marriage vows."

Mr. Truth stopped Old Man from further explaining the vows. He had questions related to the sincerity of the vows, and asked Mr. Marriage to instead sing the vows in the True Box.

Mr. Marriage was dragged by security into the box. He started hitting the box hard with his hands and his head because of the unbearable pain of the lies he contained.

Mr. Marriage quickly sang: "*I, take you, to be my partner, to have and to hold from this day forward, for better or for worse, for*

*richer, for poorer, in sickness and in health, to love and to cherish;
from this day forward, until death do us part."*

The Box echoed: *"I, take you, to be my slave, to have and to hold
from this day forward, no matter how good or bad our lives turn
out to be, no matter if I don't work hard to make enough money
for living or supporting a family, no matter how lazy and useless
I become, you are obligated to stay with me. No matter if I fuck
around and get dangerous diseases that could be contagious and
life-threatening, still you've got to stay with me without any other
options. No matter how badly I treat you, you are to be with me
until I die."*

Mr. Marriage stated that he would try another version of the
same song.

*"I, take you, to be my wife, my constant friend, my faithful
partner, and my love from this day forward. In the presence of God,
our family, and friends, I offer you my solemn vow to be your faithful
partner in sickness and in health, in good times and in bad, and in
joy as well as in sorrow. I promise to love you unconditionally, to
support you in your goals, to honor and respect you, to laugh with
you and cry with you, and to cherish you for as long as we both
shall live."*

The Box echoed: *"I, take you, to be my wife, my only friend, and
you will not have other friends, even though people change with time,
and we will not evolve, but will remain constantly unintelligent. In
the presence of God, our family, and friends, I sacrifice myself to
my solemn vow to be your faithful partner. I will remain faithful
even if you are sick, and remain the same in good times and bad
times, and now let me tell a big fat fucking lie, that I promise to love
you unconditionally, when in reality, many conditions apply. As
mentioned earlier, the conditions are that you need to be my slave,*

you need to laugh when I want you to, you need to cry when I wish you to, and you need to have a good time only when I permit you to. You need to be my slave until the end of your life."

Stage Six:
MARRIAGE GOES PUBLIC

"Enough," said Mr. Truth. He thanked Old Man for the information provided up to that point, and asked Mr. Marriage to step out of the True Box and continue explaining the next stage of his life.

Mr. Marriage was relieved to step out of the box.

He explained that as time went on, he dedicated his life to church weddings, and never stepped outside of the church. During his stay, Mr. Marriage made a few new and boring friends like Mr. Baptism and Mr. Penance.

As God wished, the church's power grew exponentially.

A few centuries later, Mr. Marriage started feeling extremely bored with the same drama and music of the church.

"I missed my power, influence, and freedom," said Mr. Marriage.

"Did you do anything to overcome your boredom?" asked Mr. Truth.

"Luckily, I needed to do nothing," said Mr. Marriage. "There was a new phenomenon on the rise that changed things forever: the power of the state."

"Ah, so it became a fight between the state and the church," said Mr. Truth.

Mr. Philosopher wrote: *There cannot be two equally powerful entities; one power will always tease and replace the other. Power never feeds on the good or bad of humans; it feeds on its own hunger. The hunger for power always leads to disturbance, and such disturbance paves the way for the future peace of a society.*

"Yes, you know all that state versus church shit," said Mr. Marriage. "As part of that power game, the state wanted to dilute the power of the church by forcing marriage to go public. Observing the power struggle, God permitted weddings outside the church to make the state happy."

"So, you were finally out," said Mr. Truth.

"Yes, I stepped out of the fucking church as a part of that transition," said Mr. Marriage. "Such a clear blue sky and such fresh air! I had missed the interesting world outside the church. But, but," muttered Mr. Marriage, "but fucking God did not give me complete freedom! I'm sure that was because God knew about my past contacts and powerful network. God ensured that even though I could step out of the church, I had to be accompanied by a priest and a few witnesses to monitor me."

Having waited patiently for a long time, God walked to the center of the stage and raised His hand resolutely. "I need to say something now. I need to."

"No, You may not," said Mr. Truth. "Let Mr. Marriage complete his statement about how You controlled things in the past."

Displeased, God walked back to His place again.

Mr. Marriage explained that even though God had permitted marriages outside the church, He had introduced a Marriage

License to closely monitor and control people. The Marriage License was a yellow paper with gold etching that read: *This is to Certify that Man and Woman were, by God, Mr. Marriage, and the church, united together in Holy Matrimony in the presence of (witnesses' names).* At the bottom of the Marriage License, written in the man's blood, were the words: *God hath joined Man and Woman together. Man cannot tear this asunder without permission from God, Mr. Marriage, and the church.* Married men and women were supposed to wear their Marriage License, rolled into a pendant, at all times. They were required to produce it when the Marriage Police questioned them.

"Did no one protest against this?" asked Mr. Truth.

"A very few leftover intelligent people did," said Mr. Marriage. "They opposed the labeling of people's statuses, and disliked the idea of an authority sanctioning paperwork for their personal lives. They protested with boards and banners that read, in black: *Don't want paper. Nothing can be crueler. We want an answer. Don't want God to be our life's author.*"

"Did that have any impact?" asked Mr. Truth.

"Of course not. The protests were mere noise," said Mr. Marriage.

Mr. Philosopher wrote: *It never works, not when the poor, insane masses hide behind God and religion. A sane person's argument can never win.*

Mr. Man was looking curiously at God, wondering how much freedom he had truly lost.

Mr. Truth said to Mr. Marriage, "Finally, out of the church, were you happy?"

"I was confused about my own happiness. I felt uneasy, knowing that once I had been the one who accompanied the wealthy and powerful, but now my company included the fucking poor, lazy, and useless. I could see that I'd made a mistake by conspiring with God and that sick bastard JC, but I was left with no choice but to sing the same song, and dance the same dance, and live the same stupid life with the same unintelligent, happy, fucked up people," said Mr. Marriage sadly.

Stage Six:
LOVE MATTERS

"Now tell me about love. How did you get involved with the 'love' factor?" asked Mr. Truth curiously.

"It was fucking God's idea, not mine," said Mr. Marriage. "God came up with a radical idea. He thought that He could blend love with religion and marriage. The thought caused God great excitement. He wanted to implement it, with the clear purpose of making me an ordinary, weak, simple man instead of a strong, strategic, wealthy man. God knew very well that love was frivolous, but if used optimally, it could be a powerful instrument of control in the name of religion."

"How about your ruler then, did he not do anything?' Mr. Truth asked.

"Mr. Past, on the other hand, having seen me as a serious subject related to wealth, strength, and power, did not like the idea of frivolous love becoming a part of me. He fucking hated the idea of love and marriage being blended under his rule."

"So, what did you do?" Mr. Truth asked Mr. Past.

"Nothing," said Mr. Past.

"Mr. Past was not able to do anything," interjected Old Man. "At that stage, God changed loyalties; he brought the young, confused Mr. Present into the picture and demanded that Mr. Past retire. He made Mr. Present the new ruler. Mr. Marriage, on the other hand, was happy with the new alliance, as he could taste love like never before."

Mr. Past remembered his words when he resigned: "*Tis not f'r love that men wilt marry, but f'r sexual desire. This desire is the wrong reason to marry. Whatev'r the case may beest, 'tis Mr. Present's problem anon. I am not concern'd. I am happy that in mine time, at least, marriage was more serious than just a vile carnal attainment.*"

Mr. Marriage added, "God happily accepted Mr. Past's resignation, as He knew how to adapt to the new generation of fucking lovers."

Mr. Truth interrupted before Mr. Marriage could explain this phase of his life, since the subject of love concerned the rule of Mr. Present, and would be discussed the next day.

Mr. Philosopher added to his book:

Marriage changes drastically as you flip the page from bad to worse.

He made the wrong friends, as I am making one in you.

Let us explore more of the Past as Marriage grows.

Horror is never fast, until you choose to close.

I cannot stop telling you a story of tears,

Since truth is all this book fears.

It was almost evening, with the sky flaunting its changing colors from clear blue to mesmerizing orange and brown. Mr. Truth announced that it was break time, and the people in the gallery started stretching their bodies and engaging in conversation while waiting for the proceedings to resume.

MARRIAGELESS

PLACES, WOMEN, AND THE COMMANDMENTS

MARRIAGE AND PLACES

After the break, the Assembly reconvened in the early evening to finish the second day of the trial. Mr. Truth walked back to the stage with his eyes steadfastly on Mr. Marriage. He walked in a straight line, and one could hear the sharp clacking of the soles of his shoes.

"Let us resume the proceedings. Mr. Marriage, please continue telling the Assembly about your life in the past."

Mr. Marriage explained that he had not only changed over time, but had also taken different forms and structures in different regions of the world. He had made his influence and left his mark in all places, including the remote ones even God did not know.

"It is unbelievable, but I was more omnipotent than God, then," said Mr. Marriage, reminiscing.

Mr. Philosopher wrote: *Who lives and survives? It is not the one who is consistent, not the one with integrity, not the one with intelligence, and definitely not the one with morals. It is the one who changes: the one who survives to change, and changes to survive.*

Mr. Marriage looked at his torn clothes, bloodstains now added to the colorful designs, and held them together. Then, in anger, he tore them more, crying out loud.

"I wore different clothes in different societies, my tongue spoke different languages, and my words had different objectives in different places," he asserted.

"Why, what was your purpose then?" asked Mr. Truth.

"In general, in many places, my mission was only to make babies."

"Just babies?" asked Mr. Truth.

"Yes," said Mr. Marriage. "But I offered very liberal ways of providing women to men in the form of courtesans for pure sex play, while wives were only for manufacturing legitimate children. Of course, wives had the added responsibility of taking care of a man's house, as well as the tool below his belly, unlike the courtesans who only needed to please his tool."

Mr. Marriage was bleeding badly, and he found it very painful to speak with his wounded mouth and bleeding lips. He started coughing and spitting blood all around him on the stage. He used his long hair to wipe his face. The blood then slowly dripped from the ends of his hair. His damaged face looked like a blood-soaked mud ball.

"You said you had different objectives in different places; please explain this," requested Mr. Truth as he opened his file to make notes.

"I am fucking tired, but let me tell you this," sighed Mr. Marriage.

"In a few indigenous societies, my objective was collective survival and getting work done together. In those regions, I worked with men who had many wives.

"There, the wives took care of the house and worked equally hard to survive. They did more than simply take care of a man's tool. Even though those regions had poor economic lifestyles and lacked glamour, they saw more gender equality."

Mrs. Woman interrupted to make a point. "I prefer to be an economically poor but equal partner dwelling in a hut, instead of being treated like a pretty-faced royal bitch whose only purpose is to simply get fucked in the most expensive palace, pop out children, and lead a life of luxury."

Mr. Marriage did not respond, instead going on to explain to the Assembly how in the East, the ancient lands of old traditions and expressionless dwarves, he was all about inexplicable traditions and scary customs. He confessed that he had taken part in Ghost Weddings, in which innocent young girls married animals, calling them devils or spirits.

Ghost Weddings were forced on a lot of girls who had been born under ominous astrological omens and were thus expected to bring death to their husbands shortly after being married. The male elders of the society examined the stars at the time of birth and declared the girls would need to partake in a Ghost Wedding. In order to avoid bringing death to any future husband, the girls were forced to marry animals and then kill them. After the animal's death, the girl was now considered a widow whose inauspicious birth circumstances were no longer a threat, and she was able to safely marry a man. However, not many men preferred to marry them, since they were originally labeled unblessed and unsuitable for marriage in those ancient societies.

"Really?" Mr. Truth was surprised. "But why?"

"Yes," said Mr. Marriage. "The purpose of these kinds of marriages was to save the lives of the little girls and their future marriages."

Mrs. Woman could not digest the fact that this had been done for the benefit of little girls and screamed, "You did this to save us? That is such a lie! I wish you had saved us from yourself and God, not from ghosts or devils."

"How about in the West?" asked Mr. Truth, taking notes.

"There, it was all about the fuck-fest within the family," said Mr. Marriage pointedly.

He explained that moving westward, it was all about bloodlines: men marrying cousins, brothers marrying sisters. He had participated in schemes, plotting against siblings, mothers, fathers, and brothers for more power. Along with political ties and the drama of bloodlines, he had helped men use wives to acquire land. At times, Mr. Marriage required husbands to marry off their wives to other men in order to gain land.

"Okay, I get it," said Mr. Truth. "And I have one more question: do you take the blame for all the atrocities committed against women? Yes or no?"

"Come on! You cannot blame me for all of that," Mr. Marriage protested. "I was, and still am, a populist. Call me the people's champion instead, exactly like God."

He laughed hysterically and continued. "I did all of it to accommodate these dumb people. I might have forced them at times, but they opted to be forced. It's not my mistake completely, not at all. You cannot hold me solely responsible; it's a collective disaster. Mr. Past, God, and all of these dumb people sitting in this Assembly listening to me are just as responsible. They deserve nothing better than dog shit anyway," shouted Mr. Marriage, coughing up fountains of blood as he laughed more.

"God is not the people's champion! Never say that," corrected Old Man.

The whole Assembly was looking curiously at Mr. Marriage, their heads pulled back and their mouths gaping open. Mr. Marriage, looking at the Assembly, shouted, "What are you dumb fucks looking at me like that for?"

A few men and women shouted back, "We all deserve to know more of your past."

"Really? All of you? All? Not just one or two?" asked Mr. Marriage, and laughed, rolling on the stage, uncontrollably rubbing his face in his own spilled blood on the floor of the stage, muttering, "This is a joke."

Mr. Philosopher penned in his book:

What do humans deserve, and what do you, as a reader, observe?

God says they deserve to serve; do you agree, or do you swerve?

Humans deserve nothing, as there is no collective human.

It's only you, an individual, thinking, who is never collective, but only one.

MARRIAGE'S BIZARRE RULES

While closing his file and capping his pen, Mr. Truth asked everyone on the stage, "Is there anything more to say about Mr. Marriage during Mr. Past's rule?"

Mr. Marriage pulled his hair back and tried to get up to exit the stage, thinking that Day Two was coming to an end. "Nothing more. I am fucking done with my bloody past. Let us call off the day before Mr. Present also starts blaming and fucking me tomorrow," he announced.

"Not yet! How about your rules, your crazy rules?" asked Old Man. "I witnessed them."

"Rules, yes, there were some rules. Yes, we made them. God, Mr. Past, and I made them together," said Mr. Marriage, not interested in explaining. But he knew Mr. Truth would make him confess, and explaining the rules would take some time, so he sat back down without anyone instructing him to.

"Do you mean God and Mr. Past also had roles in this?" asked Mr. Truth.

"Yes, of course, that's exactly the reason I have been telling you I am not the only one responsible for the whole fuck-up," said Mr. Marriage, irritated.

Mr. Past was about to respond to Mr. Marriage's statement, but God placed His hands slowly on his shoulders, restraining him from saying anything.

"Mr. Past and I are innocent. He must be lying," said God. "Father will punish you and you will not go to heaven if you lie," said God, widening His eyes and looking at Mr. Marriage angrily, but still with a smile on His lips.

"I am not lying. I am not fucking lying," screamed Mr. Marriage, crying and beating his hands against the stage.

Mr. Truth simply waited.

After a few minutes, Mr. Marriage gained some composure. He confessed that he and God had made a few rules that later became part of society's uncompromising traditions and customs.

"A few such rules that became customs were Willful Death, Red Parties, Confession Saturdays, Sweet Daughters, and, most importantly, Monthly Meetings to preach the Commandments," Mr. Marriage admitted.

Often, a convenient and fancy fictional idea becomes a serious tradition that a society decides to follow without reason and without question, wrote Mr. Philosopher.

Mr. Truth demanded that Mr. Marriage explain these traditions.

"I beg you, I cannot do it, I'm too fucking tired and weak. Give me some time," moaned Mr. Marriage, and crawled to one corner of the stage, tucking his head between his arms.

Mindful of the time, Mr. Truth requested that Old Man tell the Assembly about the traditions, to which Old Man agreed immediately.

WILLFUL DEATH

Old Man explained that according to the tradition of Willful Death, a widow was obligated to perform a funeral rite of immolating herself on her husband's funeral pyre. The most important condition was that the widow had to smile while being burned alive. She was supposed to say, "My life is part of your death. Thank you, God and Marriage, for giving me an opportunity to die as a blessed wife, knowing I was born a sinner but am now considered a winner," as her last words. She was to fold her hands together, keep her eyes open, and jump into the fire with a smile.

A woman who followed these rules without erring was

considered sacred, and became the object of reverence and worship in society. Her ashes were distributed as a sacred food to the man's relatives. Relatives and friends were supposed to eat this substance by mixing it into rice, milk, or water. The bones of the widow were to be decorated and used to adorn the hallways of her family's home.

Mr. Philosopher wrote in his book: *Humans always love their dead, but hate the same dead during their lifetimes. Death not only ends life, but also gives birth to sympathy, which later encourages love and respect, irrespective of what the person did while alive.*

Old Man explained an added clause in the Willful Death laws that required the widow produce a son before she died. If she had not produced her son by the time of her husband's death, then she was forced to marry her dead husband's brother or father. No one from outside the family was allowed to marry her, because she was considered to be family property.

RED PARTIES

Old Man realized that talking about the custom of Red Parties would disturb Mrs. Woman, just as Willful Death clearly had— the look on her face betrayed her discomfort.

"I am sorry, but I need to speak of this custom openly," he said to Mrs. Woman, and continued.

Old Man explained that a girl's parents hosted a Red Party for her after they discovered she had started her natural monthly cycle and turned from a girl into a woman. They invited all their relatives and friends to a party with red banners that read: *My daughter found her Red*. All parents were required by Mr. Law to invite Mr. Marriage without fail, and to notify him of the girl's potential to become a wife in the future.

During the Red Party, the girl was supposed to sit center stage with her head down, wearing white clothes and sporadically spilling red starches around her, symbolizing the power of her functioning reproductive system. She was not supposed to move, so as not to dirty anything with her blood. She was not supposed to look at anyone other than her mother. When others spoke to her, she was supposed to close her eyes, smile, and thank them for visiting.

Old Man explained to the Assembly that Mr. Marriage would do a quick inspection of the girl's body by running his hand all over her, as well as checking the redness and smelling it. He would then make a public announcement, saying either, "Yes, she is now ready for Man's tool," or, "No, she needs more time." If she was ready, Mr. Marriage would whisper in her ear, "You are lucky that the platform to create children is ready now. Now a man can plant a seed in you."

The girl was supposed to smile. Smiling was a symbol of acceptance. It did not matter whether the smile was forced or not; only the acceptance mattered.

Based on the outcome of his inspection, Mr. Marriage took the girl's information, portraits, and statistics, which he would share in his social meetings with all the men who were hungry for wives.

At the end of the Red Party, the girl's parents would touch Mr. Marriage's feet and ask him, "Sir, Mr. Marriage, may we offer her to you or to God? Please accept her."

Mr. Marriage, who was usually busy, often offered the girl to

God, and the parents were usually grateful to God for touching their daughter's soul and body.

CONFESSION SATURDAYS

Mr. Truth was hurriedly writing down the important points as Old Man continued on to the next custom, Confession Saturdays, without pausing.

Per the custom, after a woman delivered a child, she was supposed to stand in the center of the market early on Saturday mornings, and confess how many men she'd had sex with in her entire life.

As she recited the name of any man other than her husband, she had to remove one piece of clothing from her body. The rule permitted her to wear only one gown on Confession Saturday. So, if she had slept with more than one man (i.e. someone other than her husband), she would be naked after stating the second name. If she had slept with more than two men, then she was required to sell herself while standing naked in the market. She had to give the money to her husband as a gesture of apology. The more men she had slept with, the more times she was required to sell herself.

"Wasn't that insane?" shouted Mrs. Woman. "Can you please stop it?"

"It was insane, agreed, but let me finish; that's the only way we can expose him," said Old Man.

"Indeed, it was sick," said Mr. Truth.

"The worst is yet to come," said Old Man.

He explained that the worst part of the custom was that the woman was supposed to offer her body to the men who paid her in public, in the same market that same day and the following night, as part of her penance. If she had slept with five men in her entire life, then she had to be used by five other men who were present in the open market that same day. When men paid for her in the square, she was not an accountable human being, but instead a piece of meat or cattle to be used only as the men saw fit.

Mrs. Woman ran from the stage to one of the back rooms of the Assembly, not able to take any more. As she shut the door, she shouted, "Mankind has always thought of women as property."

Old Man continued to explain that, in many instances, women were stoned to death when they failed to complete the tradition on that same day and night. In order to fulfill the tradition and save herself, at times a woman had to run around and knock on the doors of houses, begging to be bought, even into the very late hours of the night. She was afraid of the sun rising the next day.

The worst part was that she did not have any say in how many times a man wanted to use her once he had paid. Sometimes men teasingly took their time, leaving her naked in the market for a longer period. There were a few sick husbands who encouraged their wives to have multiple affairs, because it fetched them money on Confession Saturdays.

"How about God, did He not stop this?" asked Mr. Truth.

"The merciful and almighty God and Mr. Marriage were very much part of the audience in the market," said Old Man.

"I can't help it, it was tradition, and it needed to be followed in the name of the Father," said God, while Mr. Marriage conveniently avoided eye contact by putting his face between his arms and lying down.

SWEET DAUGHTERS

"Do you still want to hear more?" Mrs. Woman asked the Assembly, walking back to the stage with tears running down her cheeks.

Child was simply observing all of this.

"We have to," said Mr. Truth, and requested that Old Man continue.

Old Man started explaining that families who were ambitious but not wealthy did two things in their lives: one, they produced beautiful daughters; and two, they consulted Mr. Marriage about whether to sell or endorse their daughters to wealthy rulers. This led to the Sweet Daughters tradition.

He explained to the Assembly that when a king or ruler visited the marketplace, he could see hundreds of fathers standing behind stools on which were placed sweets. Their daughters stood in front of them in transparent white dresses. The daughters were blindfolded with black cloths, and they stood with bared breasts and thick red color on their lips. The fathers carried boards that said: *Come to the street; take my sweets, and also my daughters.*

That was one of the easy ways for fathers to become rich and powerful. Mr. Marriage would decide the arrangement in terms of whose stool could be placed where. Selling a daughter was considered a big win, and successfully doing so helped a family gain respect.

Mr. Philosopher wrote: *It is always debatable whether fathers*

love daughters more or daughters respect fathers more. However,
love and respect are optimally exploited in the game of marriage.

Old Man continued, explaining that to earn a win for their fathers, the daughters had learned some tips from Mr. Marriage. They kept their lips slightly open and stood with their breasts turned up.

Once a man approached a daughter, her father would say, "Sir, here, I give you this beautiful woman for you to make sons with."

Then the father would eagerly wait for the man to say, "Yes, I shall buy this fruit," or "No, the fruit is not tasty."

The father would often say, "It tastes good, sir, I know it," in order to persuade a man to take his daughter.

As Old Man was explaining the custom, Mrs. Woman was looking at Mr. Marriage without any expression on her face.

"There is more I want to tell you about God, who was my brother and is now my enemy," said Old Man.

"About me? No need," said God.

"Go for it, please," allowed Mr. Truth.

GOD'S FANTASY

"God wanted to see his first fantasy of blindfolding the first woman in the garden acted out on Earth," said Old Man. "One day, God shared his fantasy with Mr. Marriage. God said that in his fantasy, he wanted to see Mrs. Woman wearing a black veil for her entire life."

Fantasizing is not just human, it's more than human, wrote Mr. Philosopher.

"God said he knew Mr. Man wanted Mrs. Woman to be treated like his property," continued Old Man. "God also knew Mr. Man would feel that his property was well-guarded and pure if Mrs. Woman was always behind a veil. God and Mr. Marriage knew that purity was what Mr. Man loved and lusted after. Mr. Man had famously said, 'Give me a pure pussy and take half of my wealth.'"

"This is blasphemy!" said God angrily. "In the name of the Father, stop spewing these venomous words out of your filthy mouth. These are all lies."

"I appreciate Your cooperation so far; You can continue to cooperate by keeping Your mouth shut, please," said Mr. Truth, showing God back to His place on the stage.

Old Man explained that as part of God's wish, Mr. Marriage had implemented a rule whereby Mrs. Woman had to wear a black veil in a few nations. In those places, she not only wore a black veil, but also was covered in black from head to toe.

God was very happy to see all women in black veils. It made Him feel that they were all identical, even though such sameness never existed in reality. God used to get furious when someone did not obey the "cover your face" rule.

"What would the punishment be if a woman didn't obey?" asked Mr. Truth.

"The Marriage Police would pour tar all over the woman's head and naked body, and cut off her ears and nose," said Old Man. "This was done in the public marketplace, in front of everyone, of course."

He continued, "Only husbands and fathers had the right to raise the black cloth and look at a woman; no one else was permitted. Gradually, a woman's objective in life became: 'Protect my pussy and give the purest to my husband.'"

"I never knew you had these kinds of dark fantasies," said Mr. Truth, looking at God and writing notes.

"You have no idea about his fantasies and his behavior with women," said Old Man. "I have seen it from the beginning."

"What did you see?" asked God angrily, confronting Old Man. "In the name of the Father, answer Me."

"In the very name of the Father, I know what you did in the garden, I know you what you did with the first woman under the tree, and I also know what you did to the Father," said Old Man.

He paused, and finally asked, slowly, "Shall we continue on that subject?"

"No, let us not get into it," said God, retreating to His place.

Mr. Truth requested that Mr. Marriage explain the Monthly Meetings, but he got a negative response from Mr. Marriage.

"No. I am fucking tired. I am too weak to talk now," groaned Mr. Marriage, which made him even more irritated and tired. He tucked his head into his arms again and did not bother to pay any attention to the Assembly.

It fell again to Old Man to let the Assembly know of the Monthly Meetings.

MONTHLY MEETINGS

Old Man related that one fine day, in one of the conversations between Mr. Marriage and an exceptional husband in the market, the husband said he loved his wife more than anything in the world. In response, Mr. Marriage asked him if he loved his wife more than he loved God and Mr. Marriage. The husband responded yes, since she made him happy and made him feel like his life was worth living. He immediately apologized to Mr. Marriage for saying such a thing, but said it was true that he loved his wife more than anyone or anything.

Mr. Marriage could not digest this fact. He shouted at the man, calling him weak, calling him a pussy, saying he wasn't even a man, and left the market. The next day, Mr. Marriage had an emergency meeting with God to do damage control. They were very worried that if women were loved dearly, it could lead to a debate about equality in society.

So, Mr. Marriage devised a new community program of hosting Monthly Meetings for all wives. In these recurring meetings, he preached the Commandments under the guidance of Mr. Past and God, and the tight security of the Marriage Police.

Old Man gave a copy of the Commandments, printed on paper, to Mr. Truth. Mr. Truth opened the papers and started reading the Commandments to the Assembly.

Commandment One:

Thy Husband is Thy King,
and Thou Must Serve Him

As a husband, man blesses and honors a woman. He gives her an opportunity to be his wife by marrying her and bringing her into his home. She must be happy to serve him, clean him, and feed him. An excellent wife gives all authority over her own body to her husband.

She must take care of the house, and in her free time she is permitted to entertain herself by weaving or singing for her husband, but only with her husband's permission. It is a man's responsibility to train her like he would train his dogs and children. It is his responsibility to make her a perfect and excellent wife, and he can use either reason or rape to accomplish that.

In exchange for his training, he has the first right to savor his excellent wife. He has the right to do anything to his wife that his dirty, beautiful mind can think of. His excellent wife is obligated by the first Commandment to follow his wishes dutifully, even if they lead to her death. If such a death ever occurs, it is called Holy Death.

Old Man added that, historically, a few husbands were good men who only plucked their wives' hair or threw burning stones on their chests as a part of their training. But many men had taken unjust advantage of this stupid Commandment.

Commandment Two:

Thou Shalt Hold No Other Person Above Thy Husband, and No Man Before God

---

An excellent wife has a hierarchy to obey in her married life. God comes first, followed by her husband. No other man or woman shall be more important than these two, until she bears sons. Most importantly, she cannot consider herself important at all. Humbling herself will lead to a truly happy married life; a happy marriage never has any conflicts, because an excellent wife is not supposed to weigh her priorities against her husband's.

The head of every wife is her husband and the head of all men is God. No one is the head of God; God is the beginning and the end, the alpha and the omega.

Man was not created for woman, but woman was created for man. A wife who hopes to earn God's favor and enter into heaven should submit entirely to her husband. At times, conflicts may arise between God and the husband, especially when it is God's turn to demand service from the excellent wife. This Commandment solves the problem by requiring an excellent wife to serve God before her husband. This is a solution leading to a conflict-free human society.

Commandment Three:

Thou Shalt Not Have Any Ambitions Other Than Serving Thy Husband

---

A woman serves, and her ambition is only to be the most perfect and excellent wife in order to make her man happy and her family successful. She takes instructions and follows them. An excellent wife's intelligence is considered nonexistent. This Commandment praises an excellent wife who admits she can never speak like her husband, handle things like her husband, be smarter than her husband, or be ambitious. Finally, she must say that she can never live without her husband. An excellent wife should learn submissiveness. No woman, even an intelligent one, should have any authority over a man. Instead, she should be quiet.

Commandment Four:

Thou Shalt Not Misuse the Name of Thy Husband, Thy King

An excellent wife knows that her husband and his name are as precious as her life. As a traveler in the desert uses his water sparingly, so an excellent wife should use her husband's name. An excellent wife is always a servant and a helper to her husband and she tries not to take his name in vain.

Commandment Five:

Remember Saturday and Sunday

From Monday to Friday, an excellent wife is supposed to labor and do all of her husband's work, but Saturday and Sunday are the days dedicated to God and Mr. Marriage. On these days, she shall do God's work. She and her husband shall not sleep together, since it is a holy time, and sex is not considered holy.

Commandment Six:

Honor Thy Father Before Marriage, Thy Husband After, and Thy Son Later

---

An excellent wife's life should be centered on three men. It is her duty to permit fathers, husbands, and sons to own her unquestionably. At times, fathers-in-law and brothers-in-law may also become co-owners of a woman. A woman should never be free. A free woman is a sinful entity.

Mrs. Woman interrupted, "Why her father? Why her husband's father? Why his brothers and why her sons?"

Mr. Truth asked Mr. Marriage to respond to her.

Mr. Marriage explained, "Fathers, because they work hard for your bread. Your husband's father, because he created your husband. Your husband's brother, because brothers share in the name of brotherhood."

"How can a mother let her son fuck her?" Mrs. Woman cried helplessly.

God proudly said, "Because he is a man, and man is blessed, while a woman is a born sinner. No rule in the world can supersede this. Man is blessed."

Mr. Truth continued to read the next Commandment immediately, so Mrs. Woman could not react to God's insensitive statement. There was not a lot of time left in the day.

Commandment Seven:

Thou Shalt Not Talk and Thou Shalt Never Say No to Thy Husband

---

An excellent wife should cook, wash, take care of the house, and love her husband. She should never question anything her husband says and she should not enquire about his work. There is an easy way to determine how good a wife is: the less she speaks, the better she is.

Mr. Truth asked Mr. Marriage to explain why there should be so little communication between wife and husband.

Mr. Marriage clumsily raised his head, which was dripping with blood, and replied, "A wife can utter a word or two in a day or a week, but as time goes by there should be no communication between husband and wife, since the wife should know what tasks are to be performed at what time."

He continued, "A man is a man, and his wife should be always available to him when he wishes her to be. A man likes to be loved, so his wife should perform such acts of love, like sucking him, for a minimum of thirty minutes every day. It is important that she say, 'Honey, you are the best, baby.'

"This is all the communication that is needed," he concluded.

Mrs. Woman jumped in again, and said about Mr. Marriage, "He was pathetic; he educated wives on happiness while explaining this Commandment. He told wives they should always submit themselves to their husbands on a bed, with their legs spread as wide as possible to make their men happy. It did not matter if it was dry."

She remembered the pain and shamefully closed her eyes.

"He always said, 'Pain is temporary, but happiness is not.' He asked wives to focus on their husbands' happiness and do whatever it took. He told them to offer their mouths or their bodies or their hands to make their husbands happy. Sometimes, husbands liked to hit, burn, and brand their wives. Wives were told again and again, 'Pain is temporary, but happiness is not.'"

"Did wives not seek out the ruler of their time for help?" asked Mr. Truth.

"It did not help," said Mrs. Woman. "Many wives asked questions, but Mr. Past used to give an example of a beautiful girl who was sixteen years old as an explanation," said Mrs. Woman.

Mrs. Woman explained to the Assembly the story of a 16-year-old girl whose father had consulted with Mr. Marriage and made her marry a powerful, wealthy, but beastly 52-year-old king. A few years later, the girl complained to Mr. Marriage about her life. She said she had been having painful nights with her husband. The king did not know her language, and they had never uttered a word to each other.

The king did only two things in life: he fought enemies in the daytime, and then violated her all night in the worst possible ways. There were rumors that everyone in the entire kingdom had heard her painful moans while the beast was violently satisfying himself. Mrs. Woman concluded the story by saying that the beastly king did not just use the girl hard and brutally, but literally chewed her entire body with his merciless black canines.

"I am still around," said a woman in the Assembly, pushing the crowd aside as she came forward from the gallery. She was bloody, her hair covering her naked body. All her skin had been peeled off and her face was distorted, her pupils invisible in her eyes. The people in the Assembly were shocked to see someone without any skin, dripping blood from all over.

"Who are you?" asked Mr. Truth.

"I am the woman you are talking about; you can call me Ghost Girl. I could not die completely, and now I want to ask questions about my marriage, and communication," she said.

"Oh, shut up. What does marriage have to do with communication, anyway?" Mr. Marriage asked.

"Marriage is all about communication. How can couples bond without speaking to each other?" asked Ghost Girl. She asked the question innocently, even with her horrific appearance.

"Oh, please. Stop that, for fuck's sake," said Mr. Marriage impatiently. "You have got to be thin and slender, possess a juicy virgin thing below your belly and a beautiful innocent face, and that's it," he said proudly.

Justifying himself, he added, "The beastly king I made you marry did not need anything more than that. He wanted you to know his name because he liked you to scream it at night while he was crawling on you. All you needed to do was get more beautiful in the daytime, and serve him at night."

The people in the gallery could not believe the insensitivity of Mr. Marriage's explanation, but he continued.

"You had an easy problem to solve. The fucking solution was that you did not need to speak with him. He did not love you. It was better that way, and I am sure you would have had a beautiful and successful marriage, and one day you would have become a successful queen with many sons, if you had not made him unhappy enough to flay you to death in public."

Mr. Truth realized that this was a good discussion; the Assembly got to hear about how Commandment Seven was used to exploit girls.

But he wanted to move on, so he said, "We will talk about you later," to Ghost Girl, and started reading the next Commandment. He knew he needed to objectively present as many points as possible in a limited amount of time, even though Ghost Girl wanted to say more.

Commandment Eight:
Thou Shalt Not Ask for Love

A husband can seek sexual pleasure outside of marriage. This is considered good for the wife, because this way she gets her space, as well as freedom from her husband's sexual demands.

Mr. Truth requested further explanation from Mr. Marriage.

"You should be happy he is fucking around with other women," said Mr. Marriage.

"A man is allowed to get a woman from a place called the Wife Bank. He can only borrow; he can never buy them. So, don't worry," continued Mr. Marriage, laughing hysterically again. "The Wife Bank loans women out and they behave like wives to men, but they come at a price."

Looking at the women sitting in the gallery, Mr. Marriage screamed, "In the end, I know you might not love your husbands, but never think beyond that. You need to know that love is another word whose meaning has been lost, which will never serve any practical purpose. But it is a fucking magical word. You need to say, 'I love you, my man,' as many times as you can, even if your husband does not respond. It's your duty as a wife to do all that I have said."

Mr. Truth now gave God a chance to talk about Commandment Eight.

"Men need sex. They are still like cavemen," said God. "They need sex with different women, and it is My will that they shall have it. You shall not have any problem with that."

God ended His explanation by saying, "As for women, the objective of sex is procreation, not lovemaking. It would be considered blasphemous if a woman sought men for sex as men seek women. That is My will, and that's exactly what this Commandment tells us."

Mrs. Woman looked helplessly at Mr. Truth as he started reading the next Commandment.

Commandment Nine:

Thou Shalt Not Give Any Testimony, True or False, against Thy Husband or God

An excellent wife shall never speak out against her husband or God, even when demanded by Mr. Law. It is her duty to favor her husband and God in any testimony, beyond the logic of good and bad, beyond the logic of truth or falsehood.

Commandment Ten:

Thou Shalt Not Leave Thy Husband Until Thy Death

Man is the only one who has the right to leave his wife. An excellent wife must stay with her husband. Her only other option is to kill herself in the dark, without blaming her husband. An excellent wife becomes the property of her husband when married, and she cannot be disposed of unless the husband thinks it is necessary.

"That is the end of the Commandments," said Mr. Truth, putting the papers in his file along with his notes.

Mr. Truth looked at Mr. Marriage, God, and Mr. Past, shaking his head with disappointment and contempt, while Mrs. Woman held her hands in fists of rage, biting her lips, clearly unhappy about the Commandments.

"Remember your answers to those wives; you will get what you deserve," said Mrs. Woman, cursing those responsible.

Mr. Marriage did not even care to respond to her.

After contemplating this for a while, Mr. Truth asked Mr. Man, "You seem to have been the beneficiary of a lot of Mr. Marriage's activities in the past, don't you agree?"

"Yes, I do," said Mr. Man. "But I did those things to abide by the rules of God and Mr. Marriage."

"Again, the same old disease of humans: blame, blame, blame," said Mr. Truth angrily. "Will you ever get tired of blaming women, or God, or someone else? Child has a reason to cast blame, not you. You are a man; own it, and behave like one."

Mr. Man said nothing, and put his head down.

Mr. Truth turned to Mr. Marriage and said, "All the rules and Commandments of the past, and your explanations to the wives, make me believe that you think Mr. Man is better than Mrs. Woman. Why do you favor Mr. Man over Mrs. Woman?"

"It has always been the case, from the first man ever created," said Mr. Marriage, and laughed. "It is fucking silly to ask me. Ask God; ask all the priests, popes, and imams of the world who are men. God is also a man. Does it make sense now?"

"So, you think God made them believe that?" asked Mr. Truth.

"Yes, of course."

"So, if you think women are inferior and sinful, will they never be blessed at all by you and God?" asked Mr. Truth.

"No, they can be blessed," said God. "Those women who follow the Commandments will be rewarded with seventy-two male virgins in heaven with full-sized, perfect cocks. Seventy-two men, all six foot two in height, with beautifully sharp eyes, hairy bodies, white skin, strong arms, and broad shoulders. These men are untouched and unbroken by any previous sexual intercourse. They have erections until the woman is satisfied, and they recite poetry beautifully."

"Really, such nonsense. How about men? What do they get for making sure their wives follow the Commandments?" asked Mr. Truth.

God explained that men would be rewarded with thirty-six virgins, all five foot eight in height, with hairless underarms and legs, full-grown pear-shaped breasts, beautifully wide eyes, white skin, slender arms, and long legs.

"These virgins with voluptuous, perky breasts and sweet-tasting pussies sing beautifully and don't have menstrual cycles," He added.

"Is this also written in *The H Book*?" asked Mr. Truth.

"Of course it is," said both Mr. Man and Mrs. Woman, nodding together.

"And do you believe it's true?" asked Mr. Truth.

"Yes," said Mr. Man, while Mrs. Woman said nothing.

45 SECONDS OF SLAVERY

Suddenly, a drop of blood fell from the sky onto Mr. Marriage's forehead. When he looked up, all he could see were the intricately carved walls of the Assembly, none of which could be dripping blood. He couldn't see all the way to the ceiling, but he assumed that the Holy Assembly wouldn't produce something so ghastly.

A few moments later, more drops fell onto his head. This time he could see the 16-year-old Ghost Girl hovering above him, surrounded by millions of other naked women with blood pouring from their scarred, stained bodies. Most of them had bleeding mouths, and a few of them looked as though they'd been beaten and raped.

Out of the millions of victims, Ghost Girl appeared out of the sky again to moan and scream. She wanted to pick Mr. Marriage up with her bloody teeth and eat him. Instead, she scowled at him and yelled, "Why did you do this to me, to us? What right does marriage give a man to treat us this way and kill us in the end?"

When he noticed her mouth was bleeding, Mr. Marriage laughed, slapping the floor of the stage.

"Even *my* mouth is fucking bleeding," he smirked.

Ghost Girl screamed, "I blame you and my husband! You said it was my duty to suck, which was stronger than his ability to shove it in my mouth. The animal in him came out and showed me how a monster can reside in the form of a husband. All of his dreadful strength came from the institutions of marriage and religion."

Mr. Truth wanted to comfort Ghost Girl, but her pain was beyond consolation.

Ghost Girl, through her bleeding mouth, sang poetically:

"I was the youngest and lived as a kid with my Granny, not knowing she wasn't my mom.

I thought I was the bravest as a kid, and nothing less than a firebomb.

All I needed to do was be the loudest and ask for what I wanted,

113

and I got all I wanted without any qualms.

I should thank and blame my granddad for pampering me and making me feel like the best; I did not realize as a kid what my future was to become.

I grew, and I flew to my mom, and I knew that I was again the darling of the home.

I was rude, without much of a worldview, yet was like the princess of Rome.

Never knew that I even needed to ask for that glass of milk, or for someone to bring me that comb.

My memories brewed with sweet lies, and all my smiles under my family's dome.

Yes, pampered again and pampered more, I thought life could never offer me one second of tears or slavery.

No, I never cared for anything more than my fun, my friends, my world, without knowing that even I would need to go down on my knees just to be free.

Married for only the reasons of society that I know of, and got a man.

Worried for a lot of long seasons, weeping on my divan.

I plead with myself now not to bother my mind, for it pains me to re-scan."

Ghost Girl stopped and screamed again loudly. She scratched her breast until it bled badly, and cried despairingly.

Mr. Truth asked, "What happened next? Tell me. Let it out."

Ghost Girl sobbed, "I remember that night; I cannot forget. Don't blame me for not pleading, not demanding. I did, and I did so strongly. But remember, I am the one with two breasts and one hole and the world knows that I am physically weak. How could I stop him, when his ears did not understand my plea? How could I stop his body, his stronger arms and legs, from overpowering me? How could I stop him, when I had no inch of this vast world to escape to? How could I stop him from removing my clothes and my skin and making me naked, not only physically, but mentally?

"How could I push away his hands, when I knew my tears had no meaning to his heart, and my cry had no meaning to his ears? How naked could I be, with both my body and mind alone and exposed in the shifting earth of all men? How much more enslaved could I be than at that moment, when I had to absorb him into me, when I did not want it to happen? How could I stop my tears, remembering how innocent I was as a kid, when I felt that I was the bravest and the luckiest? How much could I hate my family for loving me so much and leaving me here to go down under this body of meat and just take it in? I felt pain, pain that flesh will heal, but how about the part of my respect that exploded forever, making me never see myself as holy? I did wait for the moment to pass, but how could I stop it when the machine was acting on my innocent body? I felt that rhythm like a death stroke, like an earthquake. I even took it, swallowing the respect I had for myself; I took it wet, wishing I could just jump in an ocean to die. How did the cruel God know I was waiting for those forty-five seconds of slavery to end, and yet not run the time wheel any faster? And before this horror killed everything in me, I had to relive the forty-five seconds of slavery again and again.

"Now, I think back to my dear, loving parents, and I demand, I shout, I insult: Where am I, under this dark night, under this man, under this guilt? And how could I imagine the souls of my family ever seeing me in this pose? This will never be forgiven, for God had no mercy upon me."

With tears still pouring from her eyes, she disappeared into the sky along with the other women.

"Your testimony will not go to waste," said Mr. Truth, and waved goodbye to her with a pained expression.

Mr. Past, without showing any sign of remorse, said, "'Twas common in mine era, and I would not beest surpris'd if 'tis still common in the era of Mr. Present."

OLD MAN'S ADMISSION

Mr. Truth turned to Old Man. "Is it entirely true, what Mr. Marriage said of his stages and how he sinned in the company of God, JC, and Mr. Past? Say yes or no."

"Yes."

"How about the rules? Did Mr. Marriage go along with God and Mr. Past?" asked Mr. Truth.

"Yes."

Mr. Truth suddenly realized that there was one person still missing. It was JC, who had played an important role in this case.

THE LIFE AND TIMES OF JC

"Summon JC here to the Assembly immediately, please," Mr. Truth commanded God. "I want to ask him a few questions."

"He is no more; he is dead," said God, a single tear almost dropping from His right eye. "I lost my dear son. I lost him, when he was only thirty-three, in the final battle between good and evil. He sacrificed himself for all of us here in the name of our dear Father," said God, wiping His tears.

"Stop it," said Old Man impatiently. "He is lying. It wasn't a battle between good and evil. It was a scheme to have JC end his already cancerous life in the name of human sins."

"What nonsense. In the name of the Father, don't say that," protested God.

"I do remember the whispers in the woods that night," said the Old Man with a subtle smile. "When you told JC to put on a final public show, in which he would die in front of millions of people in the name of human sins."

Mr. Truth asked, "Why would God do that? And what would JC get out of it?"

"JC made money and humped women, but he wanted the legacy of his name to remain for centuries to come. God helped him, in return for what he had done for God by setting up all the churches and helping God control humans though marriage."

Old Man added, "God wanted JC to die in the name of human sins in order to make his religion stronger, and to ensure that marriage and religion became inseparable."

"But why did JC agree with God?" asked Mr. Truth, trying to connect the dots. "Why did he need to sacrifice his life for God or humans, or even his own legacy? He could have lived more than thirty-three years; he was still young," said Mr. Truth.

"JC had nothing to lose," said Old Man. "JC was already infected by the horrible things he had done in his life, and by the snakes that repeatedly bit him every time he committed a sin. Moreover, he had incurable cancer. He knew his death was inevitable. He knew he would die of the poison and the cancer. Hence, he agreed with God's plan."

"Does anyone have his photo?" enquired Mr. Truth.

God pulled one from his pocket slowly, and handed it over to Mr. Truth.

JC had long hair and a beard in the photo.

"Can you give me more details? What about his younger days? He looks like a dramatic artist in this photo," said Mr. Truth.

"Those were lost years for him. No one knows what he did between the years of twelve and thirty," responded God.

Old Man interrupted, "He was a handsome young man with a prolific sex life who drank the best wines during those lost years."

Mr. Truth contemplated the photo some more, and finally said, "Okay, let us not waste any more time on JC. He is dead and gone. Let us focus back on Mr. Marriage."

CHILD AND MR. PAST

Mr. Truth had gathered substantial case points and understood the role of Mr. Past, Mr. Marriage, God, and JC. More importantly, he understood the way Mr. Man and Mrs. Woman had been treated, but he still knew nothing about Child.

Realizing this, he looked at Child and asked, "Dear one, please come over here and explain your life in the past."

Child jumped off its chair and spoke, with guilt in its voice. "I was born, like any living thing, without reason and without sin." It paused for a moment and continued.

"But as I started growing, I was told I was a born sinner, and that my sins could only be washed away by God's holy grace."

"How did you feel when you were born? Did you feel sinful?" asked Mr. Truth.

"No," said Child, with joyous remembrance. "I felt I was born like any other beautiful flower: innocent—a winner, not a sinner."

Suddenly, its facial expression turned sad. "But right from day one, I was told that God was there and I needed to obey His commands."

"Did you like to be commanded? If not, then why did you obey the ones who told you this?"

"I was not born with God's religion or a belief in marriage," said Child, raising its head confidently. "Actually, I was born as a baby, and it so happened that I was born into a family where my

119

parents were God-believers and marriage-followers."

"So, what was the problem? Did you tell your parents the truth that you didn't believe in God, and you might not respect the belief system of marriage?"

"Yes, I told them, but they demanded that I give a valid reason not to believe," said Child helplessly. "I tried as a kid to explain, but I did not think I needed to give them a reason. It was purely an accident that I was born into a place where my dad and mom believed in these institutions."

"So, what happened?" Mr. Truth asked.

"They did not let me go out, and tortured me by reading me *The H Book* a thousand times," said Child, with fear in its eyes.

"They scared me, and said I would be fried in hot oil after my skin was peeled off if I did not believe in God and marriage. I was scared, so I agreed. I could not sleep for months, because that thought almost killed me with nightmares."

Mr. Truth did not want to pain Child any more by asking additional questions.

"Good job, kid," he said, patting Child's back.

It was late in the evening, and the humans needed entertainment and rest. The moon graciously danced out from behind the mountains and sang a beautiful song to the humans to put them to sleep:

"Sweet little children, close your eyes slowly.

The day and the sun are done, now it's time to be easy.

Think of what you've won, and sleep with silent glee.

Now, make no thoughts run, and my son, sleep now, as I count to three."

MARRIAGELESS

4

PRESENT

QUESTIONS, CONFUSION, AND LOVE

The day began beautifully with a blazing sun rising from behind the brown mountains. The sun stretched her arms with comforting rays. As the sun rose, all the people awoke, enticed by the beautiful morning light. The light brushed the dark gray Assembly with a bright golden color, transforming it into a lively sight.

The Assembly was ready for Day Three of the proceedings. The people were ready to bear witness to Mr. Present.

"In the name of the Father, did you sleep well? It is going to be a long day, but a great day," said God to Mr. Philosopher, as they both were getting on the stage. "Be prepared to write and sing a lot."

"Sure. Early mornings are a good time to begin for those who respect a good night's sleep," Mr. Philosopher answered. "I don't respect nights enough to sleep. Night has never blessed me with sleep, just as it never did for my dear friend Mr. Rational. I wait and sit patiently through the night in the company of a trusted friend of the darkness—the clock, who ticks and ticks and ticks, until the sun rises, and then I step out."

Mr. Present came over and stood by Mr. Philosopher. He was dressed in clothes that were neither completely classic and old-fashioned, nor future-friendly and trendy. He wore triple-pleated black woolen trousers that reflected some shades of past traditions, white running shoes, and a yellow crew neck T-shirt. His comfortable outfit reflected his confused yet contemporary fashion sense. He also wore green and gold classic aviator sunglasses, even in enclosed dark spaces, to avoid showing the confusion in his eyes.

Lips always lie, but eyes never do, wrote Mr. Philosopher.

Mr. Present scratched his head carefully, without disturbing the arranged stream of his hair. He got on the stage, looking more confused than ever.

Looking at him, Mr. Philosopher said, "Don't you worry; everything evolves, including God, evil, humanity, institutions, and the values of the world. Such is the nature of things against time, and so it is that the nature of marriage has evolved as well. Even though *The H Book* denies the very concept of evolution—despite it being a known and provable fact—things evolve, even if God is blind to them. Good old God should have consulted a few intelligent people before authoring that book, which he certainly must have written while heavily drunk—that is, if he had actually written the book."

Hearing Mr. Philosopher, God warned him, with a smile still

on His face, "Careful, My son, you are talking about Me. I am God, the almighty God. Don't forget that." He ran His fingers proudly through His long white hair.

"I won't forget that you are God; I cannot. You also need to know that I am not one of these obligated husbands or wives, who feel a duty to live for others, to earn for others, to sacrifice for others. I don't do any of that; I have no duties to anyone other than myself. You cannot intimidate me. Neither my death nor my philosophy holds fear; both of them simply lie in wait to be experienced as truths of their own when the time comes. A philosopher's death is always a memorable story for everyone. I would be happy if you'd like to begin that story right now. Would you, please?" said Mr. Philosopher, smiling.

God did not want to attract any more attention. Hence, He did not respond.

The judges, the witnesses, and the people were all ready to listen to Mr. Present. Mr. Truth was all set to question him. Mr. Marriage was still badly wounded and lying down in the center of the stage, waiting to see what direction his case would take.

Mr. Philosopher, looking at one of the confused husbands at the front of the gallery, wrote in his book:

Look inside yourself; even I can see your confusion.

None would know that truth, since even you know only half-truth.

You are confused between my reason and your tradition.

You are confused between my truth and your falsehood.

We both see that your life is a lie.

We both know your lie will never fly.

We both know you will live miserably and thus happily die,
Unless you discover the rest of the half-truth.

MR. PRESENT DEBATES 'LOVE MATTERS'

Mr. Truth requested that Mr. Present further explain Mr. Marriage's stage of Love Matters, which had been postponed while Mr. Past was presenting his stages of marriage on Day Two.

"Love has become the central theme between husband and wife. Thanks to Mr. Marriage and God for helping me to achieve that in my rule," Mr. Present said proudly.

"I really appreciate Mr. Marriage for transforming so greatly. It must have been a difficult journey," said Mr. Present, looking at Mr. Marriage and giving him a thumbs-up.

"Mr. Marriage has completely metamorphosed throughout time," he continued. "He went from being a serious businessman dealing in money and power to being a man of religion wearing long white robes and dealing with JC and God—all during Mr. Past's rule. More recently, during my rule, he has transformed into a lover-boy wearing handsome blue jeans and plaid shirts with rolled-up sleeves. It cannot be easy for one person to change so drastically."

The crowd that had attacked Mr. Marriage the day before began showering pity and sympathy on him. The crowd started to empathize with him, beginning to understand the transformative pain that Mr. Marriage had had to endure to make love a part of his institution and their lives.

They came to the front row and said to Mr. Marriage, "We are sorry, we really are. Thank you for bringing love to our married lives."

Looking at God, they said, "Thank You, too, God. You are always the best."

"You are always welcome," said God, smiling gracefully. "You know that all of you are My loving children, and I never disappoint My kids."

"Sure you love them; sometimes it is extreme love, like the woman in the garden," said Old Man, taunting God.

God ignored him.

Several men quickly brought over a garland of beautiful yellow and red flowers that was as tall and heavy as Mr. Marriage. The crowd ran onto the stage and forcefully pulled Mr. Marriage up from the ground. They made him stand beside God and placed the huge garland around both of them. Mr. Marriage was still bleeding badly. He looked gruesome and monstrous with his bleeding red face, his swollen eyes, and a crooked smile, in which his few teeth loosely stuck to the gums. His chin was completely broken, with flesh hanging off the bone. The people who had attacked him and kicked him with their boots felt sorry.

While the crowd was doing the garland ceremony, Mr. Philosopher said to Old Man, "Such is the nature of humans: they change their rational judgments based on the sorry state of another. A sense of empathy is a detriment to decision-making. Humans love to show sympathy, since they can never admire power in others. When they meet a person with power and potential, they undergo immense stress to find ways to feel more comfortable about themselves. It is visible when a poor person says, 'What is money? It is just paper. Peace of mind and being joyous are the keys to a happy life.' It is visible when a person who has spent his or her life following someone says, 'It is an easy job to be the leader, but I want to balance my life with my family.'"

Old Man smiled for the first time that day. Even though Old Man was the biggest champion of humans, he knew that all humans lied in the name of love, sympathy, and humanity.

Meanwhile, security cleared the stage by pushing the crowd down, and Mr. Truth insisted that Mr. Present continue explaining the Love Matters stage of marriage to the Assembly.

Gazing at the tattoos covering Mr. Marriage, Mr. Present explained that the love tradition had changed thousands of years of marital conventions, which had earlier been based on wealth and power. He said that now, the focus of marriage was not the production of many strong sons, but rather, how happily a wife and husband led their individual lives.

He stated: "Love and affection have become the standard, and this love revolution has swept in and crept to all corners of the world."

Mr. Marriage started thumping his chest, showing the tattoos *LOVE* and *AFFECTION* to the crowd. He smiled broader than his lips would permit, while repeatedly giving thumbs-ups to the people.

The humans in the Assembly suddenly started missing their loved ones. They began searching the crowd for their partners. They began blowing kisses to one another across the room. They flung their kisses, as if kisses had wings and could fly like birds to peck the lips of their partners.

One young man who had never been married ran to his

girlfriend, who was sitting in the women's section of the Assembly, knelt at the girl's feet, closed his eyes, raised his right hand, and sang: "*When the charm of her beauty comes close to your senses, that moment of wonder and life-giving experience brings joy to your ever-youthful heart. Men who have tasted this beauty can never share their joy with others, but they can live the rest of their lives with the memory of that glimpse of her charm. It's not about beauty, but it is all about the personality of that beauty. It's not her naked back and her shiny wet hair; it is the incomprehensible sight that makes her the definition of beauty, as the first man ever described what beauty was to the world. Life and death appear like two polarities between the two corners of her beauty: live with her, or leave to die without her.*"

"Did you steal my job of philosophizing and singing?" said Mr. Philosopher to the young man, laughing.

"Stop it, please," said Mr. Truth. "What you sang is called appreciating beauty. It could be love, but what does this have to do with marriage? What does it have to do with the accused?"

"You don't understand it, do you?" said Mr. Man. "At times, love and humor are more important than truth. You wouldn't understand it."

Mr. Man bowed down to Mr. Marriage in respect and smiled.

Mr. Marriage did not care to return Mr. Man's show of respect; instead, he raised his middle finger.

Listening to what Mr. Man said to Mr. Truth, millions of men and women started laughing out loud without knowing why. God started to play music, and they all started dancing without recognizing the tune. They chattered while they danced. They seemed to be saying something no one understood, but they all nodded with comfortable smiles.

Mr. Truth implored everyone, "Stop it! Stop laughing now, please. This is no joke! Let me focus on Mr. Present; I have important questions for him."

At this point, the humans seemed to have forgotten the past sins of Mr. Marriage and God. They were happy, dancing and laughing.

Mr. Philosopher wrote: *Happiness is such silly merchandise; you throw this merchandise to people and they forgive your past sins completely. At times, forgiveness itself is a bigger sin than the actions of a sinner.*

After some time, the crowd calmed down, and Mr. Truth started questioning Mr. Present.

"I have a problem understanding the connection between love and marriage," Mr. Truth said. "I understand that humans need love; it's a beautiful thing. But can love be the whole purpose of marriage?"

"Yes, love makes life beautiful. Love is everything; love is all you need," said Mr. Present, his arms crossed in front of his chest.

"As I said, I understand that humans need love, and that it is a beautiful thing. But here we are not just talking about love between individuals; we are dealing with marriage, which is a societal issue. Mr. Law is involved in it, rule books are involved in it, and the Marriage Police are involved in it," said Mr. Truth.

"I don't understand; what are you trying to say?" asked Mr. Present.

"I am not trying to say anything. I am asking questions so that we can understand the relationship between love and marriage. People need love, but might not need marriage, because it involves things like laws, obligations, and restrictions, which may or may not be in line with the concept of love," said Mr. Truth.

Mr. Past jumped into the conversation. "Wherefore not allow love to exist as a personal decree? Dost thou not agree that love be a straight and easy aim for man, as it is mere gimcrack demanding no brains nor wit nor sweat to achieve? It takes but a few cute, dimpl'd smiles, and a few pretty falsehoods to cheer the other's countenance. 'Tis the easiest thing, and hence, strong and intelligent humans might not crave it. Is love not an overrat'd conceit in the base and ordinary world of the po'r and suffering?" said Mr. Past to Mr. Present.

"So, are you suggesting that love is not required in a marriage?" Mr. Present asked Mr. Truth, ignoring Mr. Past's question.

Suddenly, the humans flinging kisses became angry with Mr. Truth and shouted, "We want love! We don't want truth! Love is forever! Truth is always a pain!"

Mr. Truth answered them. "Let me correct you for the last time. I am reiterating the point that love is a human need, for both men and women. Again, I accept that marriage needs love, but my question is whether love needs marriage. I repeat: does love need marriage?"

"I am not sure, but love and marriage are both required," Mr. Present answered impatiently, barely letting Mr. Truth complete his question.

"I get it," said Mr. Truth. "I understand why Mr. Past did not agree with God on the love issue, because Mr. Marriage was a serious and strong man with a clear vision. Mr. Past did not like to see Mr. Marriage conflated with an unreasonable and potentially short-lived concept of love; he saw the purpose of marriage not as the apotheosis of love, but as a strategic move in one's life. Mr.

Past expected Mr. Man to set goals in his life, such as conquering a place or achieving success, with the help of Mr. Marriage. Whether that vision was good or bad, right or wrong, is another story, but at least Mr. Past had a clear vision about what marriage was."

Looking around and seeing that the people in the gallery were listening attentively, Mr. Truth continued, "Being loved has now become a person's obligation and purpose in life. This sole purpose of love within the institution of marriage might not last much longer. I can easily see that a marriage with the central goal of love can be good between a husband and wife for a few years. But Mr. Marriage will run away if the husband and wife continue the same song of 'I love you' every day and night. I repeat, love between two people is a great thing, but they might or might not be husband and wife."

He commented finally, walking towards Mr. Past. "At times, humans do not have the appetite to sustain the stupidity and innocence of love for a long time with the same person, and that makes love an inadequate foundation for marriage. Please confirm that what I've said on your behalf is true," said Mr. Truth to Mr. Past.

"Aye, sir, absolutely."

Still not convinced by Mr. Present's earlier statements, Mr. Truth asked him, "Tell me one thing. With Mr. Marriage changing his focus from duty to love, are people at least happy with him during your rule?"

"I don't have an answer to that question," Mr. Present said quickly. "I don't know. I am still confused. It's true that people have needed Mr. Marriage to move away from his older, dogmatic standards to more open and liberal standards. This has been a significant change."

Mr. Present looked around at the confused faces of the people in the gallery and said, "But I am not sure if I can say with certainty that humans are happy with Mr. Marriage during my rule. I am sorry."

"When did this change from duty-based to love-based marriages occur?" asked Mr. Truth.

"It all started two hundred fifty years ago. That was when God and I decided to sketch the tattoos of *LOVE* and *AFFECTION* on his chest," said Mr. Present.

"So, it's a recent change. What motivated you to transform him?"

"It was religion; yes, religion caused me to change him. God wanted this change."

"So, it was God again," remarked Mr. Truth, shaking his head.

"I had good intentions! In the name of the Father, don't look at Me like that!" said God to Mr. Truth.

Old Man looked at God, and said to Mr. Truth, "It is always the case, isn't it? There is nothing but the devil in God, which makes men sin. He is the champion of religion and marriage, which make men follow him more than ever."

Mr. Truth took down notes in his file.

THE RISE OF EQUALITY

Sensing that everyone was still a bit confused, Old Man stepped in to explain things better, which had become his role in the trial.

"Mr. Present introduced the concept of equality between Man and Woman to Mr. Marriage during the early days of his rule, but God disliked it," said Old Man. "God reasoned that gender equality would cause a problem with Mr. Marriage, since Mr. Marriage was used to considering Man superior to Woman. He predicted that if gender equality came about, then women might not obey their husbands. He believed they would not consent to sex, and would even refuse to bear children because of their equal status, which would lead to the destruction of humanity.

"God insisted that the Marriage Police retain as much power as they had had under Mr. Past's rule. He thought the Marriage Police should be responsible for upholding the Commandments of marriage, even in the present. But Mr. Present insisted on moving forward with his goal of bringing equality to humanity," concluded Old Man, looking satisfied.

Mr. Truth patted Mr. Present's shoulders, saying, "Good job! We all appreciate your work."

Mr. Present smiled humbly.

WOMEN ARE EQUAL

God felt uneasy about the conversation about equality.

"In the name of the Father, women are not equal and never can be," announced God. He walked towards Mrs. Woman, and said, "Woman is a born sinner, and Man is who she should worship. Man is superior and Woman is inferior."

"Fuck you, God," said Mrs. Woman, with her head held high.

"Please stop that. I don't like your tone," said Mr. Truth to Mrs. Woman. Then he turned to God. "How is Man superior to Woman? Explain," he demanded.

To demonstrate the superiority of Man, God asked Mr. Man and Mrs. Woman to stand up. He pointed at Mr. Man. "Look at him, he is stronger."

Mr. Truth pointed to Mrs. Woman. "Look at her, she is beautiful, and her beauty wins over his physical strength. Doesn't it?" asked Mr. Truth.

Mr. Man hesitantly agreed.

"Look at him, he is courageous," said God.

"Look at her, she is charming, and her charm can win over his courage. This needs no further explanation at all," responded Mr. Truth.

"Men are more rational, and women are only compassionate," said God.

"That's untrue. Both are equally rational or equally irrational, and yes, women are definitely more compassionate, which

135

makes them far superior to men," said Mr. Truth, concluding his argument.

God, realizing He could not win, tried to change the argument. "Okay, let me agree for a moment that women are not inferior. Agreed. We all agree, in the name of the Father, but women still need protection."

"Yes, yes, Mrs. Woman needs my protection," said Mr. Man. "I have been the protector from the beginning, and I can make a few sacrifices. I will give up my right to slap her from today onward," he offered, as if he were doing her a favor.

"But I am telling you that I don't need your protection," said Mrs. Woman. "The truth is I am emotionally stronger than you. You know you cry more than a child within our four walls, but you always talk of protecting me outside the home."

Mrs. Woman looked at Mr. Man. They were seated side by side, and it appeared as if she were going to swallow him with her angry eyes.

"Okay, you don't need my protection," said Mr. Man, trying again to change the subject from equality to honor. "But my point is that you are exceptionally good at very few fields, though your contributions are honorable."

"What *few* fields am I good at?" asked Mrs. Woman, irritated.

"Oh, weaving, serving food for the family, and washing dishes. These skills bring you honor," answered Mr. Man. "But I earn money. I am the breadwinner."

Mrs. Woman stood courageously and shouted at him, "First, I don't like you or God deciding what is honorable for me, and second, women have also started earning money under Mr. Present's rule."

God interrupted. "Such courage you exhibit. You are not supposed to speak like a man. Did you not read the Commandments?" God stated while walking towards Mrs. Woman. He grabbed her shoulders tightly.

"I did read them, and the good news is that I burned *The H Book* a long time ago and flushed it down my toilet. The better news is that I am going to meet Mr. Law and make a few amendments to the laws of marriage, as well," answered Mrs. Woman, looking straight into God's eyes.

"You cannot. You will never be equal, because I created you and I know you very well," said God, grinding His teeth. He was about to slap her, and raised His hand. The whole Assembly was surprised to see God in uncontrollable anger.

Just in time, Mr. Truth screamed at God, "Enough! Lower your hand!"

Mrs. Woman, undeterred and unafraid, said, "Whatever, I have a list of demands," as she freed herself from God's hands and turned to Mr. Truth.

"What are they?" asked Mr. Truth.

"A man cannot beat his wife. It should be against the law. A man can propose to marry a woman, but he cannot command her to marry him," she stated, and continued before anyone could contradict her.

"I have more demands. A husband cannot rape his wife. Marital rape should be considered a crime. Husbands who rape their wives should have their names put on a list hung in the marketplace as an open insult, and it should go in their bona fide certificates so that the world knows their true personalities. A wife should no longer be legally subordinate to her husband. Finally, a wife also has the right to divorce her husband. Mr. Law and the Marriage Police should ensure these new rules are upheld."

Mr. Truth wrote all of Mrs. Woman's demands in his file.

"Blasphemy, utter blasphemy," said God, enraged. "I always knew confidence and strength in a woman was bad. I always knew that this was the disadvantage of female education. They should not read books; they should read only *My* book. Had she read only My book, this woman would have never dared to make such demands in front of so many men.

"Equality is wrong. In the name of the Father, I cannot let this happen," complained God, walking from one side of the stage to the other, shaking His head in disagreement.

"I am brave and I am equal. Do what you can to stop me," Mrs. Woman said loudly.

God was unable to hide his anger. He stopped walking and stared at Mrs. Woman with rage in His eyes. He was not going to forget or forgive. God was a revenge-seeker.

Looking at God and Mrs. Woman, Mr. Philosopher wrote:

Truth can never lie; God can never be true; Man can never be sure.

Woman is always shy, knowing her justice is due, but she has the weakness to endure.

I tell you today that she is he, and he is she.

Past said she is less, Present says she may be equal, Future might say she is more.

Can we all stop this; for once in the history of time, can we ask her, what is she?

She can see and can be free and complete you when you call yourselves "we."

MR. PRESENT'S CHALLENGE

To calm the situation and make the conversation thought provoking and engaging, Mr. Truth posed a question to the Assembly. "Can someone tell me what the definition of marriage is, under the rule of Mr. Present?"

God's anger quickly dried up and, in His enthusiasm, He jumped in to answer. "Marriage is a union between a man and a woman," He said, as if He represented all humans.

The most beautiful man in the crowd said, "Really? Oh dear, is it *only* between a man and a woman?"

"It's not just between a man and woman, it's more than that. It's definitely more than that, under my rule," Mr. Present corrected God.

"If marriage is all about love, then can I marry another man?" asked the beautiful man in the audience in a low voice, as if he were sharing a secret. "I love another man, and me marrying another man is also all about love. We are men in love and therefore are qualified to marry without believing in class, creed, gender, society, or any tradition. We believe only in love."

Mr. Past innocently looked at God, remembering his loyal service. He had never allowed marriage between two men or two women during his rule. He had followed God's rule that marriage was only between a man and a woman, and now he felt betrayed because Mr. Present was changing things. Mr. Past's struggle to uphold the discipline of the institution of marriage seemed to have no meaning in the time of Mr. Present.

"Thou madest me resign and this is what thy new ruler, Mr. Present, hath done. He hath insulted Thou and Thy book," Mr. Past said to God.

God walked towards Mr. Present and confronted him.

"In the name of the Father, I made you the ruler, but I don't think you are listening to Me or following My book."

"I am sorry, but what does the book say?" Mr. Present asked humbly, taking a step back.

God opened the book and, pointing out certain lines for the crowd, He recited from His memory, "In the name of the Father, if a man lies with another man like he lies with a woman, both of them have committed an unpardonable crime. Kill them both. They shall be put to death by cutting their cocks off and carving out their hearts.

"Their blood shall be showered upon them until they meet hell," said God with pride.

"What happened to the Marriage Police?" God demanded of Mr. Present. "They are supposed to ensure these crimes are punished, as they have always done in the past. What has happened to them now?"

Mr. Present maintained his silence.

Old Man reminded the Assembly of God's infamous act, when he killed everyone—one million people—in Odom and Omorrah, when he suspected that there were two homosexuals alive there.

He said, "Such mercy God has showered on humans. God does not like any disrespect of his book."

Mr. Truth wrote down the conversation in his file.

God responded, "I am still proud of my actions. Very much."

He looked scornfully at the crowd. He held the book tightly in His hands, as if He were going to kill all the humans in the Assembly at that moment.

He yelled at them, "If marriage is not between a man and a woman, is it between a man and another man? Is that what you all mean? Tell Me now, in the name of the Father, someone give Me an answer! It's blasphemous! A man cannot marry another man just because they love each other. In that case, some brother will marry his own sister, justifying his love for her.

"Where do we stop this? Shall we encourage incest?" screamed God, looking at the beautiful man.

There were many men supporting God, who screamed at the top of their lungs: "A woman for every man, and a man for every woman!" The screaming got louder as the fire in their voices was fueled by God's rage. These men were the majority, and their thunderous screams began to intimidate the beautiful man.

"Did you get your answer, or do you need the Marriage Police to take you to Death Mountain?" God asked the beautiful man, over the heavy screaming of many men.

"No. I still don't see a reason why I cannot marry another man, since I love him deeply, and love is all we need to get married, per the definition of marriage under the current rule of Mr. Present," responded the beautiful man.

"Okay, now, take a dollar bill out of your pocket and tell Me what image you see on it," instructed God.

"I see Your image in the background with a smile, a man and a woman in the foreground, and three sons on the bottom of the bill," the beautiful man said.

"What is written at the top of the bill?" asked God.

"*In God and Marriage we trust. A woman is for a man and a man is for a woman,*'" the beautiful man read.

"Now, with your new definition of marriage, can you ever imagine two men holding hands on this dollar bill? How about children?" God asked. "A man and a man cannot produce children. I am sure you at least know that?"

"I know. I know," repeated the beautiful man in fear, realizing that he would never be able to explain to God and the angry men, who were literally screaming in his face.

Fearing for his life, he said, "I am sorry, God. I won't say a word and will keep my mouth shut."

"If you strictly go by the dollar bill, then only a family with three sons is a true family. How can future families exist without producing any daughters?" Mr. Truth asked God.

Then he looked at the beautiful man and said, "You are not guilty."

Mr. Philosopher wrote:

The burden of the world, at times, is so heavy that the darkest and ugliest fantasy serves as peaceful pleasure to your senses. This experience has an aftereffect of guilt, but remember it is society that made you feel guilty. Truly, the thoughts in your mind are not wrong, even though they wear the cloak of sin. Remember that it pleased you so much that you want to reminisce, even when you pray. Such is the pleasure of pleasure.

INTRODUCING A BEAUTIFUL MAN

Everyone believed that the beautiful man was physically weak and always scared, but creative. Men and women like him were called Flexihumans, because of their flexible inclinations.

The beautiful man receded into the crowd and tried to hide himself from God's questions. He could still hear the crowd screaming, "A woman for every man, and a man for every woman!" He was insulted.

Mr. Truth questioned God amidst the loud noise. "There is no reason to show Your power over the weak, beautiful man. If You did not like the idea of a union between a man and another man, then why did You make these Flexihumans? Why did You make them with these inclinations, which You claim go against the rules of marriage? Why would You create such flawed humans in the first place, if You really think they are flawed?"

While Mr. Truth was questioning God, the crowd started pushing the beautiful man into a corner of the gallery. They pointed at his clothes and said, "Look at him! Look at his heels and his skin-tight jeans squeezing his crotch!"

The beautiful man thought for a moment about committing suicide in order to escape the insults and the Assembly. All the people looked at him as if he were naked, as if he didn't have the freedom to dress the way he did.

Flexihumans dressed in a way that reflected their true personalities, unlike the majority of people, who wore only what they were supposed to.

143

MARRIAGELESS

Yes, clothes make the man, as well as the woman and the Flexihuman, wrote Mr. Philosopher.

Mr. Philosopher stood and demanded that the Assembly be quiet and listen to him tell a story. He began by asking the Flexihumans not to change anything: not their lives and not their choices. Then he told a story of another beautiful man who had lived many years ago. The narration was philosophical, as always.

"There was a man who lived on the side of town where 'normal' men also lived. All his life, he was composed. As he lived his life, he was told by society to wear clothes. Society selected the fabric, fit, and model, and even tailored the clothes upon him. From that point on, he was burdened by his clothing. Later, his composure turned into an emotion: pain. He started tearing at his clothes to be free, to be unburdened. All he succeeded in doing was making his trousers look patchy and removing a few threads from his shirt. He grew old, and he lost what he had had in his earlier life: composure and weightlessness. His pain turned to anger.

"One day, he left his family, friends, and relatives and ran to the border of town so that his brothers would not come to find him. In his anger, he found a force that was brighter than the light, and it blew him and his clothes into the air. He finally felt relief from pain and anger. His composure was back, and he smiled, holy and naked. He was free. Without wasting a moment of his freedom, he turned to the other side of town, where men never lived, and ran to it as if his life were waiting there for him.

"The next day, his body was found. The men of the town dressed in their best clothing to celebrate his death, and dressed him in the clothes the dead were supposed to wear. In neither life nor death could that man avoid the clothing of society. Indeed, his life was wasted. We should learn from his story and not repeat

144

it," said Mr. Philosopher, trying to calm the crowd that was still insulting the beautiful man.

Yet, the crowd did not change; rather, they started shouting again, "A woman for every man, and a man for every woman!"

The beautiful man was still. He did not feel safe, even after listening to Mr. Philosopher. He wanted to run as fast as he could and jump from the mountains to die. Even while considering this fatal action, he still earnestly and honestly loved the other beautiful man. Fear and intimidation had little effect on his love. Indeed, it was a true love.

"You need not die," said Mr. Truth forcefully to the beautiful man. "You deserve an equal life, an equal marriage, an equal death, and above all, equal respect. You are human too," said Mr. Truth. Then he asked Mr. Future to comment as well, to provide the Flexihumans with more confidence.

Mr. Future walked downstage and put his hands on the shoulders of the beautiful man to console him and discourage him from jumping from the mountains.

"I know that in my rule, you will not just be equal with others, but in a few nations, you will be the majority. Be proud of yourself, since there are others who are incapable of loving a man like you can. They are limited, only capable of loving the opposite gender," said Mr. Future, returning to the stage.

Mr. Truth, displeased with the mess around him, questioned Mr. Marriage.

"Can you tell me now why you included love in your life and added such confusion?"

"Remember, we shifted from wealth- and power-based marriages to love-based marriages, and Flexihumans have the same fucking love in common with everyone else. So we cannot stop them from getting married, can we?" Mr. Marriage asked, looking at God.

"Do you blame God for this, also?" asked Mr. Truth.

"I don't blame Him entirely, but God is definitely part of it. He should have known that love-based marriages would lead to this. Now He cannot stop Flexihumans from getting married and singing the same stupid vows," said Mr. Marriage.

Mr. Truth asked God if He wished to comment on this, but God refused to do so.

The Assembly was splitting into multiple heated debate circles, everyone in the crowd loudly discussing among themselves without paying much attention to the stage.

"All of you, I request that you calm down," said Mr. Truth. "I will give you an opportunity to speak. I will open the case and make this a public debate as soon as Mr. Present explains marriage. Calm down now, or else security will throw you out," he said to the shouting crowd.

All of a sudden, they stopped, as they feared the security men.

Of course, the threat of physical violence always worked. Humans and animals still had a great deal in common.

MARRIAGE, NOT A BASIC INSTINCT

There was a lot of conflict surrounding the definition and purpose of marriage under Mr. Present's rule. Mr. Truth was not comfortable with the way Day Three's proceedings were progressing. He was not able to make any clear points for or against the accused. For the first time that day, Mr. Truth sat down near Mr. Philosopher and closed his eyes for a moment.

The confused humans continued blabbering in their own unintelligent way, trying to decide the definition and purpose of marriage.

"Why do they even need marriage when the definition and objective is so unclear?" Mr. Truth asked Mr. Philosopher suddenly, opening his eyes.

"Isn't that the question that Mr. Rational asked all his life, before his death? I think he saw the future," Mr. Philosopher answered.

Mr. Truth paused and looked at Mrs. Woman and Mr. Man. He knew that Mrs. Woman had suffered a great deal because of Mr. Marriage, and wanted to find out from her the reasons to marry.

"Why did you marry Mr. Man?" Mr. Truth asked Mrs. Woman.

"I married because everyone marries. I married because my father told me to marry. I married because it's marriage," she answered.

"It's not her mistake. It was a rule made under Mr. Past, that all men and women should embrace marriage and God; this rule is still applicable in my time as well," said Mr. Present. "Men and women are told that that is the nature of life. 'One is born to die, and in between, marriage happens.' They're afraid to go against the law of nature. They've been told that it is human instinct to marry, that that is how God created all humans."

"That is a sensible explanation for why everyone marries. Thank you," said Mr. Truth. But he knew the truth: marriage was not a law of nature. He knew that marriage was just another man-made institution, like any arbitrary religion. Humans need water, air, light, and bread to live, but Mr. Marriage and God are both optional for humans.

"Humans are so ignorant," said Mr. Truth.

He turned to Mr. Man. "Considering the fact that the past rules were in your favor and you're considered the strongest, why would you get married, even in cases when you did not want to, during the rule of Mr. Present?"

"As Mr. Present said," Mr. Man answered, "I was always told I should marry. I was told it was a natural instinct. At times, I did not like marriage, but I thought every brother of mine had an instinct to marry, so I married. This way, I did not stand out from my brothers as an exception. More importantly, I cannot satisfy my physical needs without Mr. Marriage's blessing, and it hurts to live an entire life without sex. We all know that I cannot have sex without marriage," Mr. Man answered.

Mr. Truth wanted to hear from Mr. Marriage about marriage being a natural instinct.

"To avoid your suffering, and before I take you to the True Box again, can you tell everyone the truth and make a confession?" Mr. Truth asked Mr. Marriage.

"Yes," conceded Mr. Marriage, raising his head. "God and

I tried our level best in the past to make humans believe that getting married was a basic human instinct and a law of nature. These dumb humans believe that, even today."

"Explain more," insisted Mr. Truth.

"Humans have instincts for hunger and sex. I do not represent an instinct. I confess, I am just the administrator of an institution that God tried to impose on all humans," said Mr. Marriage solemnly.

"We made humans believe that the 'glorious marriage cycle' is the ideal way to live and is instinctive to everyone, but it's not true. In the process, God and I created demeaning words, like 'spinster,' that make society at large feel that the married class is a better class. Insults to unmarried people have been prevalent in many societies under the rules of both Mr. Present and Mr. Past."

"So, I can have sex without getting married?" Mr. Man asked Mr. Truth.

"Yes, of course," Mr. Truth answered.

"Can you ever imagine needing Mr. Law's permission to eat food to address your hunger?" he continued.

"You don't need the permission of Mr. Law, Mr. Marriage, or God to satisfy your physical hunger. Of course, when it comes to addressing your lust, you need your partner's permission," he added, glancing at Mrs. Woman.

"Does this freedom apply to us as well?" Mrs. Woman asked.

"Absolutely," said Mr. Truth.

The crowd still looked very confused, as the truth was gradually coming out.

Mr. Truth requested a 15-minute break.

HUMAN HUMILIATION

Suddenly, there was a thundering noise, as if an army of monsters were marching towards the Assembly. As the dust settled, millions of animals became visible outside, spread out over the ground as far as the human eye could see. Different species of birds darkened the skies above. The humans, though they claimed dominance over all animals, felt intimidated, seeing the animals and birds.

Human dominance over the earth is so fragile when other species can fathom the idea of unity, wrote Mr. Philosopher.

A few lions entered the Assembly, and the biggest eagle flew down from the sky. They all spoke with one voice, saying, "Oh dominant species, super humans, this is what you call yourselves, but you are the weakest species. You need the help of society, like brothers, relatives, mothers, and fathers, to determine your mate. We have such pity for your species. We are braver, as we choose and live by our own terms in our partner selection. Such pity on you. More the pity that you can only sleep with one partner in your life due to your human laws. This human law goes against natural laws."

With that statement, the lions and the eagle laughed, and left the Assembly.

Mr. Truth asked everyone to focus back on the case.

"Do you want to talk about Marriage University during the rule of Mr. Present?" Old Man slowly asked Mr. Marriage.

"No, I am not talking about that fucking shit. Just leave it," shouted Mr. Marriage.

Mr. Truth insisted that Old Man tell the Assembly about Marriage University.

COUNSELORS COUNSEL MARRIAGE

Old Man explained that with the addition of equality and the flimsy concept of love, many couples struggled to stay loyal to Mr. Marriage under Mr. Present's rule. They were confused by the expectations and responsibilities of marriage. They asked questions like, "Is there any standard criterion of marriage that is applicable to everyone?" and "Is love the only requirement?" Most of the time, the answers varied from one couple to another, even though they had the common element of being married.

"Mr. Marriage has been under tremendous stress during the rule of Mr. Present," Old Man said. "Husbands and wives in the present build their marriages on the central theme of love, and at times, love is short-lived. They cannot leave the marriage, and this leads to loveless marriages. Couples have to spend a ridiculous amount of time and money to make their marriages successful, and their efforts are often insincere.

"In short," he summarized, "they put a lot of hard work towards making their marriages happy, at the expense of their individual happiness."

Many men and women in the gallery looked uneasy, as if Old Man were speaking uncomfortable truths about them that they didn't want to face.

"Meanwhile, at the beginning of Mr. Present's rule, Mr. Marriage lost his rich and powerful contacts of the past," Old Man continued. "And so he came up with a new revenue model that was sophisticated and educational."

Old Man went on to describe how, under the rule of Mr. Present, Mr. Marriage had set up Marriage University, along with many marriage counseling centers that were affiliated with the university. Men and women could enroll in the university as couples, where they were taught by Mr. Marriage, in person, to solve the issues between husband and wife.

The courses had names such as *How to say "I love you" when you don't* and *How to successfully lead a happily married life when your marriage sucks.* These were the top courses offered by Marriage University.

When couples graduated, they became certified Counselors. Mr. Marriage stamped the word *Counselor* on their tongues, so that they could speak exactly the same language and offer consistent solutions certified by Mr. Marriage. Counselors were sophisticated, and they spoke the language they'd learned in the *Marriagictionary*, which had been published by Mr. Marriage.

Counselors taught other people how to love their spouses. They taught them how to fake orgasms, and how to travel with their spouses twice a year without getting irritated. They also taught people how to dumb down their intelligence to make their spouses feel important. Counselors always reminded their students of the concept of equality, all the while knowing that the partners in a marriage were not equal.

Old Man concluded, "In the age of Mr. Present, when love is the central theme in a marriage, telling the truth becomes an unpardonable sin. This is unanimously agreed upon by all Counselors and their clients. This is what Marriage University is all about."

Mr. Philosopher added in his book:

In the world of these loveless marriages, which I call "failed marriages," people who decide to fulfill their obligations and stay with the marriage don't live; they die every day. The thought of their certain, final death offers them the comfort that their burden will end one day. That one day is the day on which they don't end their life, but rather, start their freedom in death.

Mr. Truth took down the information that Old Man had shared. He needed some time by himself, so he insisted on an extended break and went into one of the back rooms of the Assembly, along with Mr. Philosopher, who had been chain-smoking cigars. He knew very well that he had a lot to cover on Day Three, and yet he had not been able to gather a lot of information.

As he stepped inside the room, the entertainment started on the stage of the Assembly, with music and dancing. The crowd relaxed, getting involved in the music.

Mr. Truth closed the door behind him to gain a moment of peace.

MARRIAGELESS

5

PRESENT

DIFFERENT PEOPLE, DIFFERENT PROBLEMS, SAME EVIL

Mr. Truth felt better after a few minutes' rest in the back room. He returned to the Assembly, and the entertainers disappeared with his entrance. Mr. Philosopher walked with him to the stage and said softly, "In the new rule of Mr. Present, patience is not a virtue; it is a lazy man's smart excuse. People believe in quick death and slow life; they believe in quick visual learning rather than slow reading. People don't have a lot of patience for listening to speakers. It's time to open the debate to everyone and make it interactive."

In the process of making the discussion open, Mr. Truth wanted to answer a few questions and give people an opportunity to speak. He requested that the people who wanted to ask questions come to the front row and wait for him to point at them. He also instructed their respective spouses to stand with them.

A few people came forward from different parts of the Assembly and stood obediently in front of the stage in a straight line. The big screens hanging across the front of the Assembly showed the person who was speaking, so everyone could see him or her. There were also speakers affixed to the walls that broadcasted loud enough to tremble the Earth.

"Do I get anything in return for asking a question?" asked one of the men who formed the line.

"What do you mean by 'get anything'? I do not understand your question. Please explain," said Mr. Truth.

"I mean, I mean," fumbled the man, "any prize money, or some reward for asking the best question."

Mr. Truth was annoyed with that response and about to say no, when God hurriedly interrupted.

"Yes, yes, you will get a reward. You will get a surprise gold brick and a holy white shawl—used by Me—and a holy water packet," said God, who was always finding ways to make people love Him more.

"Oh really? We will be lucky to get Your used shawl and water," said the man, as tears of happiness ran down his face.

Mr. Marriage looked at the man who had asked about money and prizes.

"Fuck you," said Mr. Marriage, and added, looking at God, "God! Why don't You give them Your underwear and some spit instead, they will be happy to lick that as well. These guys would eat their own shit for thirty seconds of fame on the big screen," he said, hysterically laughing and rolling on the stage.

Mr. Truth demanded that Mr. Marriage stop laughing, and pointed at a woman who was in the front of the line, indicating that she should start with her question.

MY LADY AND MY FANTASY

The woman introduced her husband, Mr. Liar. "We have been married for sixteen years," she said. "Here is my problem. It usually happens around ten p.m., when my husband and I do the thing."

"What thing?" asked Mr. Truth.

"The thing that people do at night to please their physical senses," she answered shyly, and continued. "Recently, while he was in his usual rhythmic flow, I asked him to open his eyes and look at me."

"Did he open them?" asked Mr. Truth.

"No," she said. "My husband has been closing his eyes for many years while he performs his duty to make love to me. I had always been curious why, but had never before doubted his loyalty. Not until he refused to look at me for a long time."

"Okay, what did you do then?" Mr. Truth asked.

"I met with Mr. Detective, who offers his services to doubtful spouses like me by obtaining the *Thoughts and Dreams Report*."

The *Thoughts and Dreams Report* logged all information about individuals' thoughts and dreams in real time. Detailed descriptions of a person's thoughts, both visual and audio, were available as an add-on service on top of the basic report—at an additional cost, of course.

"I got my husband's report from Mr. Detective," the woman

explained, pulling the report out of her bag. "And to my surprise, the report detailed that he has been fantasizing about a lady named Miss NotWife for almost fifteen years. I looked into the details, and discovered that every night from ten p.m. until six a.m., my husband has been thinking about her but using my body."

Mr. Truth enquired if she had taken any action. She confirmed that she had contacted Mr. Marriage for his advice on the matter. "He visited me, along with God, and they told me to keep this a secret," she responded.

"Why? Why keep it a secret?"

"I was told that people would start doubting the fundamental foundation of marriage if I raised such questions. They told me that this was prevalent, that a vast majority of people do exactly the same as my husband was doing," said the woman.

"Is it true? Did you give such sick advice?" Mr. Truth asked Mr. Marriage.

"Yes, I did, but correction: it is not sick advice. The beauty of marriage is that people like Mr. Liar still love and respect marriage so much that they don't mind lying to their wives. His lie is a fucking sign of loyalty toward marriage," Mr. Marriage replied.

The woman raised her head and asked Mr. Truth, "Is it fair for my husband to do this to me?"

Instead of answering her, Mr. Truth turned to Mr. Marriage and God. "Did you really advise her to live a lie?"

"Yes, it is true, humans fantasize. But it is just emotional cheating to use his wife by fucking her body when Miss NotWife is in his head," answered Mr. Marriage, still defending himself.

"But my husband says he truly loves me," interrupted the woman.

158

"That's tricky," said Mr. Truth. "He might love you, but he might not be happy with you, physically. The truth is, humans are still primitive about a few things, and marriage stops them from being their true selves," said Mr. Truth.

"In that case, do you advise me to tell him to sleep with Miss NotWife to clear his head?" asked the woman with a doubtful expression.

"I would say yes, provided sex is all he wants from Miss NotWife, and not love," said Mr. Truth. He concluded his conversation with her by saying, "Thank you for bringing this to our attention. I really appreciate your courage."

Mr. Truth moved on to another woman, who was waving her hand and smiling. Interestingly, she wore a T-shirt that said: *I am perfect; see it, and measure it.*

MRS. PERFECT BY MARRIAGE

"I am Mrs. Perfect," the woman said. "You can see that I am statistically perfect." She tilted her hips and pouted her lips.

Looking at her, Mr. Marriage slowly ran his right hand down into his semi-torn boxers, while using his other hand to prop himself up off the floor.

"What perfect statistics are you talking about?" asked Mr. Truth.

"Don't you see? Look at my height, bust size, and booty curve. I am the perfect wife for any man," she explained, tossing her hair back and looking at him sideways.

"How is beauty the only parameter for marriage?" asked Mr. Truth, holding his head in irritation.

"You sound very innocent, Mr. Truth. Isn't it an unspoken truth that men want to marry women who fit the basic standards of beauty?" she said, running her red nails along her breast. "Mr. Man and Mr. Marriage made these rules, and women are meant to grow accordingly," she said, bending forward to flash more cleavage.

"What are these rules?" asked Mr. Truth.

Mr. Marriage, who was looking at Mrs. Perfect's cleavage, begged, "Hey darling, can you please hold mine and rub it. It's all up, hungry and waiting."

"Please remove your filthy hands from your trousers and maintain decorum," demanded Mr. Truth.

Instead of obliging, Mr. Marriage flashed his tool and rubbed it openly, as an insult to the whole Assembly. Security quickly ran to the stage and hit his hands with iron rods, then forcefully tucked his tool inside his boxers.

Mr. Truth insisted that Mrs. Perfect continue.

Mrs. Perfect listed the rules of attractiveness for women: no facial hair at all, minimum 5'8" tall, long fingernails, small feet, long neck, big firm breasts with nipples pointing out at an angle of twenty degrees, firm round buttocks, heart-shaped ass, flat belly, and long thin legs.

"Good for you. So, what is your point, other than claiming to be Mrs. Perfect?" asked Mr. Truth, getting bored with the conversation.

"My point is about my pain. I am in great pain," she said, and started weeping.

"But you are Mrs. Perfect. Why are you in pain?" Mr. Truth asked.

"Because none of it is real," she said sadly. "I had to get my body stitched in various places, my face puffed up, and my lips permanently stained. Now my whole body is in pain. I fear one day my skin will peel and suddenly drop off, leaving my organs to collapse."

"So, your perfect body is not natural?" asked Mr. Truth, surprised.

"Of course not. In order to conform to the beauty rules, I was measured, cut, and stitched," she said, revealing her scars.

"Tell me, dear almighty God, sometimes I wonder, did You really create humans?" Mr. Truth asked.

"Yes, in the name of the Father, I did, and I still do," said God.

"If that is true, and if You create everyone in Your own image as stated in *The H Book*, then why is there such imperfection? Why did You not create everyone equally to conform to Your standards of beauty?" asked Mr. Truth.

God just shrugged and didn't answer.

Mr. Truth turned to Mrs. Perfect's husband and asked, "Knowing that it is very painful for her to look like this, do you really need a wife who possesses only beauty, seeing as it will all fade away with time?"

"Of course I need my wife to be beautiful," answered the husband, hugging Mrs. Perfect from behind and kissing her cheeks, licking her tears.

"Understood. The question is: do you want her to be *only* beautiful, or do you need her to have other qualities, like

161

intelligence and rational thinking?" persisted Mr. Truth.

"Beauty will be sufficient for me," the husband said, kissing Mrs. Perfect on her swollen lips.

Irritated by the man's response, Mr. Truth asked, "Are you buying a lady for one night, or for life? What about intelligence? Doesn't intelligence matter to you?"

"It doesn't," the man responded plainly.

Old Man stepped in, and said, "Women are taught to put their physical appearance above all other qualities. They are taught to cultivate their bodies, keeping a few important goals in mind: to work out more, eat less, bind their feet, and do anything to enhance their beauty. If, for some reason, women cannot naturally achieve these goals, they visit the Plastic Market, where they get bodily replacements and modifications—at a cost, of course."

"Do people really go to this market?" asked Mr. Truth, surprised.

"Oh, yes," said Old Man. "The Plastic Market is really growing; everything is possible there, for a cost—the cost of losing yourself and becoming someone else. The procedures are bloody and painful, but at times women have no choice. The societal demand to be perfect is much stronger than their pain under the pins and knives in the Plastic Market."

Old Man then explained a few services offered at the Plastic Market:

FatSucker sucked all the fat from beneath the skin. The specialist in the Plastic Market attached vacuums to customized boning knives, which he drove under his patients' skin. Women who chose this procedure lost consciousness just by seeing the knives stuck into their naked bodies, and the blood that flowed out.

NoseShaper made the nose bigger, smaller, thinner—however a woman wanted it, per the image she showed the specialist in the Market. The specialist used smoothing hammers and chisels to hit the nose and make it perfect. Most of the time, the bones were powdered first, to make the job of shaping easier.

The most popular service, *BoobPlasty*, enlarged the breasts with artificial dust. Specialists cut open the breasts like cakes, and threw in expanding yellow dust to fill them up.

BagKiller eliminated bags from below the eyes. Specialists injected green liquid into the eyes and pressed hard to remove the bags. This procedure had blinded a few women as a side effect.

EarCuts was a simpler job, in which specialists chopped off the ears and stuck new ones on with special gum.

Mr. Truth was irritated at the thought of the Plastic Market, and pointed to the next person in line in order to move on to a new topic.

LOVE MORE

"I am Mr. Two," the next man said. "I am a hardworking and honest man. Because of these qualities, I make plenty of money. Actually, I have a question for God, Mr. Marriage, and Mr. Present."

"Please, go ahead," said Mr. Truth.

"Can I marry two women, if the women both agree to marry me?" Mr. Two asked pointedly.

"Of course not," Mr. Present said. "Neither *The H Book* of

God nor the rules of marriage allow such a thing. That idea goes against even my new-age thoughts."

"Why not?" asked Mr. Truth. "He is wealthy and he can take care of two women and their children. More importantly, the two women have no problem with this arrangement."

"No, it's not good. It will cause imbalance to human society. In the name of the Father, we cannot let this happen," said God.

"Untrue. This way, society will become more economically stable and prosperous," said Mr. Truth.

"It's unfair," said Mr. Two, responding to God. "Everyone knows that God has 9,999 wives, and with all due respect, He is still, um... um... forget it, I don't want to say anything against God."

"What? What did you just say?" said God, angrily walking towards him at the edge of the stage.

"Complete your thought, Mr. Two," said Old Man. "You meant to say that God is still jealous of any man like you who wants to have more than one wife. That's true. Such is God's small heart and nature."

"Did you consult anyone, like Mr. Marriage, about your situation?" Mr. Truth asked Mr. Two before God could object.

"I approached my ruler, Mr. Present," Mr. Two said.

"What did he say?" asked Mr. Truth.

"Mr. Present told me the solution was to leave my wife and marry the other woman, but I was unhappy with that solution, as my wife has absolutely no problem with my having a second marriage," Mr. Two said.

His wife, who was next to him, nodded in agreement.

He continued, "I thought it was a family matter and did not want Mr. Law or Mr. Marriage, or even God, to decide my private life. But if I follow the rules, I will either have to give up my wife or the other woman, and I will miss either of them badly."

"Equality, everyone is equal," said God. "There is no additional privilege for the wealthy and hardworking. In my eyes, the rich are the same as the poor, a hard worker is the same as a lazy person, and a giver is the same as a taker."

Ignoring what God had said, Mr. Truth suggested, "If you love both women, and if you want to decide your life, then why do you need to marry and invite complications in the form of Mr. Law, the Marriage Police, and God?"

Mr. Two paused a moment and said, "I accept what you say. It's my mistake. I don't need to get married." But he quickly realized his error, and added, "But the rule says that people have to get married in order to live together. If the other woman moves in with me and my wife, the Marriage Police will arrest me."

"I will look into this matter of living together without getting married," said Mr. Truth.

Mr. Philosopher wrote about how Mr. Two missed the woman who was not his wife:

Can I ever tell her what it is like?

I know the answer: I will never succeed.

The craving to miss her and to be alone is unhappily sweet.

The moaning of my voice with my tears falling down is unusually melodious.

Can I ever understand what is sad and what is happy?

Can we ever run towards light when there is no darkness?

How can I ever not love her when she is always near my heart?

How can I ever live without her when I don't even know how to die without her?

Mr. Truth pointed to the next man by the stage, who was smiling broadly.

MR. HAPPY WHISKY AND HIS CONTRIBUTION TO MARRIAGE

Mr. Truth beckoned the man to come to the stage and introduce himself.

"I am Mr. Happy Whisky, a businessman, and today I demand justice," he said to the crowd. "If not justice, then at least I need some credit, but all I get is abuse," Mr. Happy Whisky complained, with a broad smile still on his face.

"That's not true," corrected Mr. Philosopher. "There is one person who credited all the happiness in his life to you, and never abused you at all."

"I know; he was a good man, my good friend. I can't forget Mr. Rational," said Mr. Happy Whisky, removing his hat in respect and saluting the sky in Mr. Rational's memory.

"You want credit for what? Abuse?" asked Mr. Truth. "May I also know who approved your business please?"

"My business has been endorsed by both Mr. Marriage and God," said Mr. Happy Whisky, taking two bottles from his pocket and raising them so the people could see them.

Many people in the audience cheered when they saw the bottles.

"Why would they both endorse you? What's in it for them? Please explain," said Mr. Truth.

"Not many couples can afford the fees for the Counselors who graduate from the prestigious Marriage University. Mr. Marriage would not agree to lower the prices for counseling. Instead, he and God introduce troubled couples to me," Mr. Happy Whisky answered.

Mr. Philosopher took a new cigar out of his case, and confirmed, "I know this person quite well. Mr. Happy Whisky is a solution to a problem, but he also creates a problem that needs a solution. He has served all classes of society without any bias. He serves them all, but under different labels and vintages."

Mr. Philosopher remembered the song that troubled men and women would sing when they needed Mr. Happy Whisky, and wrote it down in his book:

For once, I hate my life.

For love, I don't deserve any.

For life, I don't know myself.

For society, I am a blot.

For my family, I am hated.

For my mom, I am dead.

For once, I wish I were dead.

"Is it true? I cannot believe God and Mr. Marriage would ever stoop this low," Mr. Truth asked Old Man.

"Yes, it's true," said Old Man.

He explained that Mr. Marriage called Mr. Happy Whisky to meet these distressed married men and women. Mr. Happy Whisky served them all, regardless of age, creed, caste, religion, or social status. He kissed all of them. Troubled spouses would smile as Mr. Whisky crawled into their stomachs, leaving a few hard scratches on his journey.

Old Man continued, "One important tradition Mr. Happy Whisky has always followed is to say, 'I kill you, but I do care' as a disclaimer. He says that every time, and ensures people are aware of the disclaimer before passing their lips."

Mr. Happy Whisky nodded in confirmation. "I do not want anyone to choose me as an obligation, or to blame me later," he explained.

"Mr. Happy Whisky is such a darling that no one can say no to him, despite the disclaimer," said Old Man.

Mr. Happy Whisky added, "People always ask for more, and I am always happy to serve them when their pockets bear gold and silver. I am generous in accepting credit or loans, but I never offer a free service. Taking me into their stomachs and brains always makes troubled married men and women feel lighter. I make them either cheerful or sad, but both emotions help. People love emotional drama, and I happily accentuate the drama."

"Good for the people who use you," remarked Mr. Truth.

"Now, humans blame me for playing this role, and they insult me by calling people who love me 'Whiskyholics,'" said Mr. Happy Whisky, unhappily opening one of his bottles and gulping some of its contents down.

"So, what do you need now?" asked Mr. Truth.

"I need respect and honor. I give comfort to so many couples.

I've earned money, but now I need respect," said Mr. Happy Whisky, who then finished the entire bottle and said loudly, "I am better than God and Mr. Marriage. The truth is that Mr. Marriage causes people pain, and God's religion does not succeed in addressing that pain. I am the real savior," said Mr. Happy Whisky, now guzzling from the second bottle.

Mr. Philosopher smiled and wrote about Mr. Man and his drinking habits:

It always took courage to maintain my resolve against this.

As always, I tell others that I hate it.

It's a lie; the truth is I love its kiss.

I cannot imagine anything that serves better when it hits.

It's considered bad for the body, a sin to the senses, and ill to manners.

So is the case with your God-directed life.

My problem is not you, but how to stop this addiction.

Mr. Happy Whisky was getting drunk. Mr. Truth decided it would be a good idea to shift the conversation away from Mr. Happy Whisky, so he pointed at the next person in line to ask a question.

The crowd wanted to hear more from Mr. Happy Whisky, but they did not want to say it out loud. They continued patiently listening to the different questions.

MR. LAW AND MR. FREE

"I am Mr. Free," the man said. "I have a problem with responsibilities and legal obligations. Hence, I cannot agree to the terms and conditions of marriage and God. I cannot get a lawfully accepted wife."

"That's fair enough. Individuals are different, so what is your problem? Is your problem that the Marriage Police are forcing you to get married?" asked Mr. Truth.

"Yes, that is one of the problems, and I remember you addressed it by promising you would look into the matter of the Marriage Police. But I have one more problem, and I need to give you some background information before I can state it," Mr. Free said.

"Go ahead," Mr. Truth said.

"I have this quality of love, and I have it in abundance. I have this ability to love many people at the same time. I was told that I was gifted that way," Mr. Free explained.

"Good to know, now tell us your problem," said God.

Before Mr. Free could continue, Mr. Marriage interrupted. "Let me tell you this: you cannot have sex without my permission, and I only give my permission if you wed the woman. You cannot be free to have sex with, or love, or wed many people."

"I cannot have sex with the same woman for more than a few months," Mr. Free responded. "Also, my freedom crosses the boundaries of gender. I am bisexual, and I like having both male and female lovers," he added, without any inhibitions.

"I am incapable of being responsible and faithful in the long term, so I cannot wed one woman or one man without letting that person down. More importantly, sex is a most primitive need, like hunger. I was born with this; all humans are born with this. It is the most unnatural and inhuman law to regulate sex. Something has to change, or else the part of my body below my belly will constrict, and I will die soon," said Mr. Free.

"How can you say this so openly?" said Mr. Present. "Are you not afraid of going against the world? Watch out, you might be dragged to Death Mountain by the Marriage Police before you next wake up."

"No," said Mr. Free. "I've never felt that it's easy to go against the world and society. I love my world. Fear is the bastard who scares you more than death; death is the friend who always tells you that he can wait for you, and there is no rush. I love my death, he is the sweetheart who can never leave me, unlike my life, who will definitely leave me one day," said Mr. Free.

"Now you sound exactly like Mr. Philosopher," said Mr. Truth.

"Indeed, free will and philosophy should sound the same," said Mr. Free, smiling.

Mr. Truth finally said, "The following are the rights a human is born with: the right to speak, the right to eat, the right to work, and the right to have sex. We need to change a few rules of marriage, obviously. It would be unnatural to make a lion eat grass, or a cow eat meat. It's the same with humans. They need to make love and satisfy their carnal hunger, but that requires permission only from their partner, not from Mr. Law or Mr. Marriage or God."

Mr. Free, like Mr. Philosopher, was very poetic. He closed his eyes and sang a song, imagining his sexual experiences. "*That*

*moment of voluntary slavery when a free mind goes down to touch
the element of impurity is an experience of the most giving and the
most selfish. It is only your friend, tender and unhappy, warm and
cold, pained and pleasured, bleeding with the pleasure of nature. I
kiss her; I kiss my friend and weep her tears. I lay myself warmly
to embrace her and see her closely. I breathe with her and kiss
her again with blood on my lips. I love the sensuality of the way
my friend locks herself up initially, and then gradually grants me
freedom to explore her. I move close to say, 'It is okay to have this
unusual friendship,' then, trusting me, she breathes easy and lets
her life and glow out, only to discover that this life is taken and
savored by me in no time. In these moments, when I see her eyes
way above, the beauty of peace makes the science and measure of
time and space hang around my neck, elevating my mental ability
to know that this is the living and real God of my life."*

"Your problem has some similarity to that of Mr. Two. Point
taken," said Mr. Truth, and moved on to the next person in line.

God was getting bored and a bit anxious, as He could see
couples talking openly and reasoning, but He could do nothing
to stop them.

THE WORKER AND HIS QUESTIONS

"I am Mr. Proffy. I work hard. I work hard," the next man said.

Mr. Proffy looked exactly like all the other professionals in the
Assembly, who worked for corporations like slaves. They were all
dressed the same, in blue dress shirts and black pleated trousers,
with short hair and clean-shaven faces. There were millions of

them in the Assembly.

"Okay, Mr. Proffy, how are you doing?" asked Mr. Truth, taking out a new paper for notes.

"Very well, how about you? Thanks for asking," Mr. Proffy said, responding professionally, his voice emotionless, his eyes blinking frequently, his smile pasted on.

Mr. Truth was surprised to hear such a formal response, and doubted the genuineness of Mr. Proffy's answer. Walking to the corner of the stage, he asked Mr. Philosopher, "Who or what is this person? He sounds like a robot."

"He is a professional; people like him work under an illusion of growth and dedication to corporate goals. Their discipline, loyalty, and consistency make them live like dead stones. Interestingly, there is a growing class of humanity, called the mindless middle class, which is made up of people like him," answered Mr. Philosopher.

The Assembly screens displayed all of the professionals at once, and they all smiled in unison. An immediate thought occurred to all the professionals as they saw themselves onscreen: the thought of being unhappy and incomplete. They realized they were all the same; their actions just imitations of each other's. They all smiled at the cameras, but could not stop Mr. Truth from seeing the vacuum deep inside each of them.

Looking at Mr. Proffy's smile, which was nothing but plastic, Mr. Truth asked him to step into the True Box. Then he asked Mr. Proffy again, "How are you doing?"

"I am bloody tired of acting," said Mr. Proffy. "I cannot do it any more!" he screamed. Mr. Proffy did not know why he had reacted that way, since he believed he led a happy and perfect life.

As he stepped out of the True Box, he continued to explain. "I work from nine a.m. to five p.m., no more, no less. I text, 'I love you, honey' to my wife every two hours while I'm at work. I get home at 6:00 each evening. I smile at my wife at 6:01. I kiss my kids at 6:02. I am told I'm a proud married man in society."

"Proud! Good, I am happy that you take pride in your life, that's good," said Mr. Truth.

"I make my parents and my in-laws happy. I am a professional with a good work-life balance, and I am told I lead a perfect life. My perfect life is made complete by getting married, so I have Mr. Marriage to thank," Mr. Proffy concluded.

"So, what is your point?" asked Mr. Truth impatiently.

"Mr. Marriage is a good guy who made me complete, and there are millions of professionals like me in blue shirts and black trousers who think the same way. My point is that Mr. Marriage is good; he completes us. Without marriage, I would be incomplete," Mr. Proffy said in his signature monotone.

"What do you mean by 'complete'?" asked Mr. Truth.

"I mean I was born on time at age zero, went to school on time at age three, and at the age of twenty-eight, right on time, I got married. At the age of thirty-two, I had children, right on time—like all the other professionals," Mr. Proffy explained, while checking that his shirt was tucked in and smoothing his trousers. "I feel complete and accomplished because of the things I have done on time. It's only because of the agreement I signed that I've been able to do it all."

Mr. Truth was getting irritated with the slow pace of Mr. Proffy's explanation. "What are you actually talking about?" he asked. "What do you mean by 'do it all,' and what agreement are you talking about?"

"The marriage agreement I signed when I married my wife," answered Mr. Proffy.

"What about the agreement? Please be more specific," asked Mr. Truth, trying to be patient.

"There are a few terms and conditions in the marriage agreement that everyone signs on their wedding day," Mr. Proffy said. "I brought a copy of the contract. Here, would you like to see it?"

"Please," said Mr. Truth, taking the document from Mr. Proffy. He sighed with the relief that he could read it instead of having to listen to Mr. Proffy's robotic voice any longer.

The contract read:

__Stage 1:__ People must get married by the age of 30 at the latest. A female must get married by 27, or else she will be socially humiliated.

__Stage 2:__ The newly wedded couple must go on a honeymoon. There, they must have the greatest sex of their lives. There are many cases of traditional or arranged marriage where they may have just met each other for the first time, but nevertheless, they must have sex.

__Stage 3:__ The couple must ensure they exhaust their physical hunger on their honeymoon, and from then on, they need to love each other forever, until the end.

__Stage 4:__ Four to five years post-marriage, the most important task of making babies is required.

__Stage 5:__ Once you have babies, you must think of money. It's all about wealth management at this stage. By the age of 40, you should have a stable job. It does not matter whether you are happy or unhappy. You need to feed your family and pay your bills.

Stage 6: *By the age of 50, you must buy a house to ensure your wife and kids have somewhere to live. By the age of 80, you must ensure you have paid off the loan on your house in full.*

Stage 7: *By the age of 90, you must say, "I love you, my wife and kids," before you die, and also thank God and Mr. Marriage for giving you an opportunity to live and marry. This is an important action before you sign off from the world.*

"Interesting conditions. What happens if you die before the age of ninety?" asked Mr. Truth. "The timing of death is never certain."

Mr. Proffy did not wait to think and respond. He had an answer ready.

"If one dies earlier, which one is not supposed to, then one needs to ensure his wife has an insurance policy that pays her. It does not matter if one has enough money to pay the premium. It is the man's responsibility to safeguard the future of the family. Businessmen sell these bonds and policies all over the marketplace. These businessmen cash in on the idea of sweet death," Mr. Proffy explained perfunctorily.

Old Man said to Mr. Truth, "The fact is that all the businessmen who make money on these insurance policies pay a portion to God, in the belief that death is in the hands of God."

"Point taken," said Mr. Truth. "Let us get back to Mr. Proffy."

"This is why I say Mr. Marriage makes me complete," said Mr. Proffy. "He sets the plan for my entire life."

Mr. Truth smiled, amused by the idea that marriage could complete a person, and said to Mr. Proffy, "I have always felt that an individual is absolute and complete, and does not need anyone

176

or anything external to make him whole. There are thousands of inspirations around him that might complement him, but a human is not an incomplete mind or body that needs fillers or supplements."

Mr. Truth sensed these professionals must be happy doing something, so he asked, "What do you like about your life?"

"I love my work, but I am told that I should love my family more," Mr. Proffy answered.

"So, you must be happy."

"I am told that I am complete, and that thought makes me happy."

"But are you?" asked Mr. Truth.

Mr. Proffy answered, "That's exactly my problem. I am not happy."

"You have been lying to yourself. You've been told you should prioritize your family, that your work is only meaningful because it supports your family. Think about it: on average, you spend seventy to eighty percent of your time at work, and you cannot say you love work more than your family. You are unhappy because your first love is your work, even though you've been told it shouldn't be," answered Mr. Truth, supporting the man's passion for his work.

Mr. Philosopher smiled at Mr. Proffy and wrote:

When the dark evening breeze hits marriage, the sun is almost setting. When day and night mutually exchange their duties, few men look at the face of marriage without a question. Marriage tells these men, "It's okay. It's okay, you can survive in marriage through this night as well. Endure until tomorrow morning, and the morning will bring you the chance to escape into your profession."

The people in the Assembly were enjoying the conversational portion of the proceedings, as most of them could relate to some of the people who were asking questions. It was getting darker, and Mr. Truth was happy, as he was gathering a lot more information from these couples than he had been able to from their confused ruler, Mr. Present.

Mr. Truth pointed at an old lady who was standing without a partner. She held a cane, which acted as her third leg.

AN OLD LADY AND HER FAMILY

"I am an old lady. I have done everything in the name of family, duty, and legacy. I have a question for you," asked the old lady, shaking a bit.

"Please, go ahead," said Mr. Truth.

"Is it wrong of me to expect my daughter to beget sons for the continuation of the family name?" she asked.

"It depends. But that does not sound like a problem statement. Please give me some more information and context please," requested Mr. Truth.

"My daughter does not get along well with her husband, so I am insisting that she have a child in order to add stability to her life and make her marriage successful," the old woman said.

"Are you concerned about the stability of her life, or something more than that?" Mr. Truth asked. "The way I see it is that you want to save her marriage. More than her individual stability, you want to make her obligated to her marriage with the help of children."

The old woman didn't answer Mr. Truth, but started ranting about her daughter instead.

"I blame my daughter for her failed marriage because of her immature attitude. She does not respect the third Commandment, which clearly tells a woman not to be ambitious. My daughter *is* ambitious, and thinks she is too smart for her husband. But she is wrong. I chose her husband for her myself, when she was young. He is a family friend, and I gladly gave the responsibility for my daughter to him. She should be grateful. Isn't my daughter wrong, as she thinks she is better than her husband, and that this is a problem in her marriage?"

"Yes," said God, "that's against the first, second, and third Commandments."

The old lady continued to rant, not even paying attention to God, and requested of Mr. Truth, "I want you to advise her. Tell her she is wrong to think she is better than her husband, and that she is wrong to trivialize marriage. I want her to do the right thing."

"Life is, at times, beyond good and bad, or right and wrong. It is true that the life of a person, irrespective of gender, is more than just marriage and customs," said Mr. Truth to the old lady.

Mr. Philosopher said, "There is no such thing as a universal right or wrong; only true or false. Facts cannot be changed, but what is right or wrong is, at times, a silly question. It can become a personal question. While there is no generic purpose to life, if your daughter finds a purpose in activities other than marriage, then she is doing great. But, if you ask me, whether she is right in doing so is not a question for me, you, or anyone else but her to decide."

The old lady looked unhappy with Mr. Philosopher's words.

"I can appreciate your efforts at passing along inherited ideas," said Mr. Truth, "but definitely not at the cost of spreading your daughter's legs to make babies. It is foolish to think that kids can possibly add stability to her already unhappy married life."

Before the old lady could respond, he added, "She does not need to take the blame for you; you married her off at an age when you certainly knew her level of reasoning did not qualify her to make a decision. You know you made the wrong decision for her, and you feel pressured to continue making decisions that are correct according to the social system in which you live, but wrong for her. However, you cannot ask your daughter to stop being ambitious and smart. In short, you cannot ask her to be unintelligent like yourself and follow what you did fifty years ago to fulfill your dreams. She is a separate entity with gifts and talents of her own. Please leave her alone," requested Mr. Truth.

The old lady was not happy with Mr. Truth's response. She still dreamt of a grandson popping from between her daughter's legs sooner rather than later. "All I am asking for is a normal life for her," said the old lady angrily.

Mr. Philosopher was amused by the phrase "normal life." He wrote:

This makes me reconsider the meaning of normal, when human life is exactly the opposite of normal. Mechanical rules should be applied to human-made things, not humans themselves. Asking for a normal life is like asking to be an inhuman construct that lives life in monotonous tones and dies a mechanical death. You need to not be human to be normal.

Seeing that no one was speaking up to agree with her, the old lady snapped, "Whatever!" and walked back to her seat in the crowd.

Mr. Truth moved on to the next person.

A DUTIFUL HUSBAND

"I am married to this woman because she comes from a family of wealth, manners, and reputation. It is a marriage that everyone calls an 'arranged marriage,' because it was orchestrated by my parents and my entire family. It is also true that I did not have much of a say in it. Now, after twenty years of marriage, my wife tells me she does not love me, and she doesn't expect love from me, either," said the dutiful husband, who was standing with his wife, as well as his parents and in-laws.

"Did she ever tell you that she loved you?" asked Mr. Truth plainly.

"No, she did not. She's been consistent in saying that she could never love a man like me, ever since the first year of our marriage," the husband replied.

"Do you love her?" Mr. Truth asked.

"I am not sure," the dutiful husband said. "But we don't fight a lot. We don't speak a lot. I think we are okay. Our families get along very well."

"Do you want to leave her?" Mr. Truth asked.

"I thought about it, but I cannot make this as a personal decision. It has to be a family decision. So, it is not easy. Moreover, my family has a traditional song."

The entire family sang the song, in unison:

"A true love is a dream

A true love is never a reality

Obedience and obligations are real

Freedom is evil

Freedom is impractical

Freedom is not good

Obligation is good

Obligation is sweet

Obligation is my life and I will never leave my partner."

"So, what is your question?" asked Mr. Truth, interrupting their singing.

"Should I expect love and affection from the woman I have been married to for the last twenty years?" asked the dutiful husband.

"Truly speaking, your expectations are unreasonable. You don't drink water to be thirsty, you don't kill a man to give him life, and you don't care for someone to hurt them. When you married this woman, you married because of her wealth, family reputation, manners, and obedience. You did not marry with an expectation of love, did you?" asked Mr. Truth.

"I did not, but I thought love would evolve within our marriage over a period of time," the dutiful husband answered.

"Not necessarily," said Mr. Truth.

The family was surprised.

"What you can expect from your arranged marriage is money, status, and respectful behavior, at best. You can also expect your wife to be dutiful and obedient to you, because these qualities were part of the agreement when you married her," said Mr. Truth. "Now, where did love and affection come into the picture? I don't discourage you from pursuing them in your marriage, but you are not entitled to a love-based relationship with her."

The dutiful husband, not convinced by Mr. Truth's answer, posed one more question.

"When you look at the younger generation, they marry based on their love quotient. But don't you agree that their marriages have not seen either the success or the longevity of traditional marriages?"

"Bravo! Bravo! Good question," called Mr. Past from the corner, and applauded.

"Yes, that's true, and rightly so," said Mr. Truth. He added, "The love-based marriages are not as successful as marriages of the past, or the present-day duty-based marriages like yours."

He paused a moment and stated, "But it is important to consider what a successful marriage is. Is a marriage called successful only if one is married for many years? Is that the yardstick that measures a marriage's success? Or is it the value that marriage adds to one's life? A marriage might not last for many years, but can entail experiences that enrich one's life.

"Marriage should make a person stronger and more independent, not weak and dependent. Good institutions make people happy; they don't make people suffer, like your marriage has," said Mr. Truth.

The dutiful husband and his family looked thoughtful, but didn't have any more to say.

"Let's move on to other questions," said Mr. Truth.

MRS. GUILTY AND MR. DEPRESSED

Next was a couple; each spouse looked sad.

"I am Mrs. Guilty," the woman said. "I have lived all my life thinking about others, and I feel pained when I hurt them. But at the same time, I make mistakes, and I have repeated these same mistakes again and again throughout my life. I am very active, and I love the outdoors. I married Mr. Depressed, who is nothing like me. He sits in one place and watches television, and that is his life all day. We are completely different, and we don't complement each other like other couples."

"Why did you marry him in the first place?" asked Mr. Truth.

"I married him because he wanted me to, and he cried when he proposed. I didn't want to hurt him, so I agreed," answered Mrs. Guilty. "I know it's my problem, but I need a solution. I don't love my man, and we both know it, but I cannot leave him."

"But why? Why can't you leave him?" asked Mr. Truth.

"Because we've been married almost fifteen years, and he has taken good care of me. He has given me money and time when I needed them. But we both always knew that we were not meant for each other. Also, there is the tenth Commandment, which does not let me leave him."

"How is your sex life with him?" asked Mr. Truth.

"We don't do it a lot. I don't have fun doing it with him. And I end up having an affair every other year. Every time I have an affair, I tell my husband I need to leave him because I cannot do this any more. The past fifteen years have been exhausting."

"Why do you have affairs?" asked God.

"Because my married life is so banal, and I like men who read poems for me," Mrs. Guilty said.

"Why didn't you leave Mr. Depressed and go to a man who writes poems? Is it just because of the Commandments?" asked Mr. Truth.

"Not really; every time I talk to Mr. Depressed about separating from him, he cries and tells me things will be okay. We both know things will never be okay. But I don't dare to step out of our marriage and see him hurt," Mrs. Guilty answered.

"The longer you stay, the more you are going to hurt him. The more time you spend with him, the guiltier you will be. The more you think of his pain, the more pain you will give him," Mr. Truth said.

"So, what should I do?" Mrs. Guilty asked.

"Mr. Depressed, why don't you leave your wife?" Mr. Truth asked Mrs. Guilty's husband, who had stood next to her, looking down at his shoes, this whole time. "She seems to be okay with leaving you. Why are you doing this to yourself? Why don't you leave her, since she keeps hurting you?"

"Because she is a lovely lady, and she is full of life," Mr. Depressed said. "My friends and relatives come to my home only because of her. If she leaves me, I won't have a life. I don't have any confidence. I will be depressed again."

"How do you feel about yourself when she is with you? And how do you feel about yourself when you are away from her?" questioned Mr. Truth.

"I feel confident when she is around," Mr. Depressed answered. "When she dresses pretty and walks in front of my friends, I like it when they compliment her. In her absence, my world is nothing. I don't have a life."

"In reality, you know you don't deserve her and it is very selfish for you to do this to her, right?" asked Mr. Truth.

"No, it is not. I always forgive her; I give her anything she wants. I would do anything for her," claimed Mr. Depressed.

"Okay, if you would do anything for her, then leave her. That's what she wants. If you truly love her, then you will not hesitate to leave her for the sake of her happiness. You know very well that she will have a better life without you. You forgive her infidelities not because of your forgiving nature, but because you don't have a choice, and this is part of your selfish scheme. I am pretty sure that if you were in her place, you would have left your partner a long time ago. Society might never understand what you are doing is heinous, but you know it for sure. What you are doing is the cruelest, most selfish thing."

Mr. Truth turned to address Mrs. Guilty again. "Relationships need to be honest. Again, there is nothing right or wrong here. There is only true or false. The truth is you don't love him, is that correct? A marriage should be based on the truth, not what is considered 'right.' Your husband has successfully made you think of yourself as bad and made you view him as good. But that does not matter. This is not a business deal where you owe someone love, like you would owe him money," explained Mr. Truth.

"What is unfair is very subjective, and only you can decide what is fair for your own life. Some will say it is unfair for you to leave him when he has done so much for you. Some will say the marriage is unfair for you, since he is not letting you go, despite knowing you are not in love with him. There are tremendous differences between sympathy, empathy, pity, and love. If you want love in your life, leave him. He needs to man up," said Mr. Truth. "And now, it's time to move on."

Mr. Truth thanked everyone who had participated in the question session, and asked them to go back to their seats. He mentioned the reward that God had promised to give to the person who asked the best question, with a pointed glance at God.

"There was no best question; they were all different questions. So, I cannot decide," said God diplomatically. Not wanting to disappoint the crowd, God threw a few of His old shawls and some water into the crowd.

The people loved it.

MARRIAGE AND THE NEW INTERNET CONGLOMERATION

While everyone obediently went back to their seats, a man crawled from the crowd towards the stage. Only his head, chest, and torso were visible. He had no arms or legs. He crawled using his head. He put his chin down on the rough ground and pulled it back to move his body forward. Every time he did this, he scratched his chin badly, causing it to bleed. He had no hair left, and his chin was swollen and bleeding. He was called Head Crawler.

"What happened to you?" asked Mr. Truth. "You look weird; where are your arms and legs?"

"I used to be a tall, handsome man, and now here I am, lying on the ground," the man explained. "I am a victim of the new age of the Internet Conglomeration."

"Internet Conglomeration? What is this, Mr. Present? What is happening under your rule?" asked Mr. Truth.

"It's a long story," answered Mr. Present.

He explained that from the beginning of his rule, he had encouraged humans to be intelligent and open-minded. This encouraged humans to start asking questions and becoming intellectual. In the process, they started moving away from religion and marriage, and towards personal development and happiness. This was a huge shift from the past, when millions of people were killed in the name of God because they had questioned the way things were. Gradually, more and more humans were becoming increasingly intelligent, with the help of their natural curiosity and the inborn chips in their heads, which had started operating. God told them not to question and to put faith first, but forces opposite God, like Old Man and his allies, encouraged them to question, to doubt, and to discover.

Old Man said, "It's true," and explained that he had watched humans living in caves, inventing fire and language, becoming skilled in hunting, forming societies, making businesses, and exploring the possibilities of life. Their greedy curiosity extended all over the Earth and entered the water and the sky. They invented and discovered, and made themselves the creators of many things.

"Humans have indeed tried to become Gods under the rule of Mr. Present," said Old Man proudly.

"That's good to know, but how is this all connected to Head Crawler?" asked Mr. Truth.

"Hold on, you will get it," said Old Man. "A few years into the rule of Mr. Present, God felt he was in the same place as he had been in the distant past, when he had less control over people. At least in the past, he had JC to consult, and Mr. Marriage to reach out to people on his behalf. But recently, people had become more independent and started questioning everything. God felt an urgent need to do something to regain control. He could see that people didn't fear *The H Book* as much they had in the past. He could not introduce a new institution to society, since a few people were already questioning the existing institution of marriage. God needed to come up with a new concept that people would like and feel empowered by, and at the same time would allow him to maintain absolute control."

Mr. Truth offered God a chance to explain. "Tell us what You did. You never confess to anything, but You expect everyone to confess in front of You. Tell us."

"I did nothing. Whatever Old Man is saying is baseless," said God, sitting in His chair patiently, as if He had no clue what Old Man and Mr. Present were talking about.

Old Man continued. "It was God, yes. Not many people know it, but God invented the Internet Conglomeration."

The Internet Conglomeration appealed to people; it made them feel free and fair. But in reality, no part of it was true; everything was virtual. Even God's close aides, like Mr. Past, Mr. Present, and Mr. Marriage, were unaware that God had invented it. It was more radical than the transformations from the Stone Age to the Bronze Age to the Iron Age.

"I thought I was thy most trusted confidant; why didst thou not tell me?" asked Mr. Past, disappointed.

God turned His head away and closed His eyes, acting like He was praying.

"Holy motherfucker, so it's You, the inventor of the Internet Conglomeration. Lovely," laughed Mr. Marriage disrespectfully.

"Shut up, it's not Me. In the name of the Father, please stop accusing Me," said God, His eyes still closed. "You are the accused, not Me. Let Me continue to pray."

"Humans live under the illusion that they invented the Internet Conglomeration, and they have started living in virtual reality," remarked Mr. Philosopher.

"If God won't tell the truth, I will," said Old Man, and continued to explain. "This new phenomenon was publicized as a tool for helping one's fellow humans, but has become more dangerous than the worst tyrants in history. The difference is that, unlike a tyrant with a thick black mustache and a growling voice, this new phenomenon does not have a human form, nor does it look scary. This non-human form has the sweetest voice, but also the most destructive mind.

"In the past, tyrants, in their totalitarian pursuits, monitored people's lives in order to gain control and take away basic freedoms. People knew their freedom was never free; it was an honest and accepted form of slavery that demanded unconditional love and loyalty to the tyrant. But now, in Mr. Present's rule, the phenomenon of the Internet Conglomeration has drastically changed everything. The enslaved don't even know they are slaves, and if they do, they don't know to whom they are enslaved."

The Assembly was in shock. They all looked at God and wondered whether to believe what Old Man was saying.

Old Man continued, "In the past, when Mr. Marriage made a deal with God, Mr. Past, and JC, he was allowed to read the stupid terms and conditions. But now, even Mr. Marriage does not have a clue about how to deal with the Internet Conglomeration. It is, first of all, a non-human form he cannot talk to, or get to sign a piece of paper. But at the same time, it can take on the form of a human, an animal, or a new life form. It can speak any language. This new Internet Conglomeration is watched over by Smiley Clouds. Every human under the rule of Mr. Present gets pleasant messages every day that say, '*Smiley Clouds love you.*' The Smiley Clouds have no real knowledge of human experiences, but they can imitate them exactly, from love to hatred to happiness—even complex human experiences, like orgasm or motherhood."

"It's all about the choices we make. Why don't people simply not subscribe to this Internet Conglomeration?" asked Mr. Truth.

"People do not have a choice," answered Old Man. "They cannot unsubscribe from the messages of the Smiley Clouds, as they cannot throw away their Eye-Phones, which are attached to the backs of everyone's hands. A few people have tried to fight against the new age and not carry Eye-Phones. One such man was Head Crawler. He refused to carry the device, and cut off his own hands to be rid of his Eye-Phone. The Marriage Police then affixed one to his leg. He screamed, 'Freedom is my birthright, and no Eye-Phone can take it away!'

"He failed, as the Eye-Phone was then affixed to his chest. Now, he cannot remove it from his body. This is how the Internet Conglomeration is related to Head Crawler."

Mr. Truth, along with all the people in the Assembly, looked shocked. Most people loved their Eye-Phones because they made life convenient and made them feel freer. They had not known God was using these handy devices to track and control them.

"Can we stop this inhuman idea of the Internet Conglomeration?" asked Mr. Truth.

"I think it is out of even God's control," Old Man said. "Moreover, it is advancing by itself at a rapid pace. It has spread quickly because it offers to help people."

Mr. Philosopher said, "Seeking help is always a signed agreement of slavery."

"How difficult will it be to stop it? Why don't you think we can stop it? We have not seen anything like this anytime, anywhere, under any rule," said Mr. Truth, surprised.

"No," answered Old Man. "In the past, at least there were cameras and screens, which had a defined range of surveillance. There were a few smart humans who could avoid someone watching them, but now with the Smiley Clouds monitoring everyone through their Eye-Phones, no one can avoid the Internet Conglomeration. It is even rumored that in a place called Area 2.51, the best scientists in the world have been working for decades to make a human born with an Eye-Phone already attached, straight out of the womb. The experiments are still going on."

Old Man continued to explain the Internet Conglomeration, and Mr. Truth listened attentively, learning many new things.

The Internet Conglomeration had many virtual rooms that people could visit. There were rooms like Sex Me, which had no windows and required you to provide your passport details to prove you were old enough to masturbate. There was also the Gossip Here room, where you could attempt to become dumb and feel happy about it. Additionally, there was the News room, where information from around the world was arranged. Finally, there was a room called Search Me, where users could ask questions and receive information. Even the Search Me room was tightly monitored, Old Man explained with a bitter chuckle, and the answers it gave were designed to indirectly control people.

Every morning, along with the artificial *Good morning and have a great day* messages from the Smiley Clouds, married people received *The One-Minute Love Program*. This program provided all husbands and wives with video messages from the Smiley Clouds that imparted new tips and tricks to keep love alive in their marriages. The messages were updated every day and were tailored to the age, gender, and personal preferences of the user. It was all about personal experience in the world of the Internet Conglomeration.

The One-Minute Love Program acted like an injection of a medicinal substance into a dying marriage, keeping it alive longer. If the program wasn't entirely natural, at least the tips helped spouses behave a little better. Over time, people began to rely on this program more than on themselves or their partners. Everyone knew that *The One-Minute Love Program* was a super duper hit that changed and saved lives.

Mr. Truth was beginning to understand there were many facts that might not appear directly connected to the case of Mr. Marriage, but nonetheless had a big impact on the outcome of the trial and the future.

God opened His eyes when He realized that the discussion of the Internet Conglomeration had ended. It was already very late.

Mr. Truth was content with the information he had collected on Day Three, even though the day had started with mess and confusion. Mr. Philosopher and Mr. Truth walked into one of the back rooms to smoke, and Mr. Truth said, "Tomorrow, it's future time."

MARRIAGELESS

FUTURE

TIME, PREDICTIONS, AND THE GODLY DEADLY FUTURE

ONE AND ONLY TIME

On Day Four, the Great Assembly was quiet. The sound of the wind passing through the vast open spaces and ruffling Mr. Philosopher's long robes was all the assembled crowd could clearly hear. As Mr. Truth took the stage, his footsteps rang loudly in the dead silence.

The people in attendance had not slept at all the night before, because they were so anxious about what Mr. Future would say. It had been the first time in their lives that they had not slept in the dark. The code had been broken. They were physically exhausted and their eyes were red, but they were attentive as they watched Mr. Future take the stage.

Mr. Philosopher rolled his sleeves up to his shoulders, smoking one cigar after another as he scribbled quickly in his book:

195

We are coming to the end; it's already future time.

Hey, are you still reading and not able to guess the crime?

It is coming, with a lot of pleading and bleeding.

It will put an end to one sick regime.

Just get ready, my dear reader; prepare for the flood of blood.

The story of all actors will be washed on the altar in water and mud.

Mr. Philosopher knew he had only one day left to finish his book.

God no longer looked confident. He was scratching His head of white hair with His long fingernails, and looked irritated. He was frowning, and His tired eyes seemed to be sinking into His face. He was not praying any more; He was worried about Mr. Marriage's future. Mr. Marriage might have been rude to Him at times during the proceedings, but God knew that he could still be a great ally in the future, provided he was acquitted.

Mr. Marriage, for his part, was no longer bleeding; he was looking at the judges and Mr. Truth, waiting anxiously with his hands clasped. He hoped to be acquitted, since he had told the truth. And he was hopeful God would rescue him if he were convicted.

Unlike Mr. Present, who was still confused, and Mr. Past, who was still obstinate, Mr. Future seemed at ease. He had already gathered a great deal of information about the history of Mr. Marriage and his influence on human society during the rules of Mr. Past and Mr. Present. Mr. Future thought he was in the best possible position to decide what would be good for the people under his rule.

Mr. Philosopher said to Mr. Future, "People love sympathy, but a lack of empathy leads to better judgment. People always doubt their pasts by saying they could have done better, said something different, or chosen a different way. Such is the nature of human regret, to live in the past and waste the present."

"Agreed. Look at them, they are very worried," remarked Mr. Future, gesturing to the people in the Assembly.

"It's not the inevitable wrong deed that worries people, it is uncertainty and the unknown that puts them in the dark and troubles them at night. The nature of knowing puts their minds at ease, even if it is the knowledge of their deaths. Knowing is a relief, but not knowing is the reality and beauty of human life," said Mr. Philosopher.

Mr. Future was friendly and confident. He was not tall and fat like Mr. Past, or muscular like Mr. Present. He was simply fit, with well-rounded features, as if space and time had shaped him into the perfect form to survive. He was wearing a light blue slim-fit shirt with gray fitted trousers and brown wingtip shoes. His face was larger than the other men's faces, and his eyes were bigger than normal. This may have appeared unusual to most people of the present, as his features were due to evolution that hadn't occurred yet. He had wavy blond hair, which moved beautifully, as if it were smiling with every step he took towards the podium. He appeared to know exactly how he looked to others, as if he knew the outcome of every step he took. He moved like a natural extension of the Assembly stage, as if he belonged there. Everything about him looked natural.

Mr. Future began clapping gaily as he walked towards the podium. He said euphorically, "Dudes and Dudettes, you should know me by now. I am Mr. Future. Along with Child, I am one of the judges. Now, let us begin the show without wasting any more time."

The people in the Assembly remained patient and quiet, eager to hear what Mr. Future would say.

He continued, "What can I say, really? What can I say of Mr. Marriage? First of all, we are not passing any judgment today. That's tomorrow. Today, let us have a casual chat. What do you say?" he asked Mr. Truth.

"Yes," said Mr. Truth. "Today, you could use your predictive analysis skills to tell us about the possible futures of marriage in your rule," suggested Mr. Truth.

"Let us start now, dude," said Mr. Future, looking at Mr. Truth.

"'Dude'? Really? Stop using that word, please," requested Mr. Truth.

"Come on, dude, you know me. I cannot be courteous like you, adding 'please' to every possible sentence," said Mr. Future. "I cannot speak the language of dead old English like Mr. Past does. The future will be casual, without any polish, with none of the finery of Mr. Past's time."

"Of course, I apologize; now please talk about Mr. Marriage," said Mr. Truth. "Don't talk about Mr. Past; he wasn't glorious, and he is clearly furious at your statement about him."

Mr. Future flashed a friendly smile at Mr. Past, who glowered at him. Then, addressing the people, Mr. Future began to talk.

"Okay, let's get started. I always wish to give you humans hope: hope that tomorrow can be better, regardless of how today is. But I am afraid, at times, to give you any hope, since it can be misleading and misinformed. You should know we cannot change anything that has happened in the past, but at least we can look at possible futures and take action today."

Child raised its hand, got down from its chair, and walked towards Mr. Future.

"I know no one asks this question because it is silly, but I want to know: why can we not change anything about the past?" it asked, its mouth open innocently.

"Because it is the past; it is all over," Mr. Future said. "One cannot go back in time to change the past. You will understand when you grow up," he explained, smiling.

"But isn't time like distance? If I could move from this point to another, why can I not move from this present to the past?" asked Child.

"Dear Child, knowing you smart kiddos, you will definitely travel back in time through a hole to kick God's butt someday, but for now, let me tell you the nature of time. Mr. Time is a lazy but strict dude who never wants to be reminded of what he has done in the past," said Mr. Future.

"Can I please see him, Uncle Future?" asked Child.

"Of course, look up: there is Mr. Time."

Mr. Time, the fourth dimension man, was hanging from the roof of the Assembly. He was round, and he wore glasses with clock faces for lenses. His skin flashed with the times from all the different time zones. Though he was always naked, one could never see any part of his body, since his two natural arms always covered him entirely by constantly ticking around his own body. He never slept and never blinked. He looked eager for every coming second, and he died with every passing moment. Mr. Time was the most powerful being present at the Assembly; even God was scared of him. But Mr. Time was also the guiltiest person in attendance. He regretted every second of his life, and hence, never wanted to revisit any past moments. In short, he was

199

forward-looking and adventurous, but hated to visit the past.

"Will he really not change at any cost?" asked Child.

"No, he'll never change," said Mr. Future. "Allow me to tell you a story about Mr. Time to illustrate my point. Once upon a time, the wealthiest and most powerful man in the world lost his son in an accident. His son was his only heir, so the father begged Mr. Time to go back to save his life. In return, the man promised to give Mr. Time anything and everything. But Mr. Time had no empathy; he was stubborn and never agreed to go back.

"He was also the only one in the world who never showed a bias towards rich or poor, tall or short, gods or demons, men or women, sons or daughters," continued Mr. Future.

"His duty was to tick and move time forward, and he did not care about anyone. He let the wealthy man's son die. To this day, he continues to let humans die at every moment, without any trace of mercy. Any time anyone visits him, weeping, and asks to go back in time, Mr. Time always says, 'The show must go on. I will force it to happen.' It would be a better world, had Mr. Time been more merciful and let a few good people live forever," Mr. Future concluded.

Then he looked up at Mr. Time, and with a cheerful wave, said, "Dude, why don't you introduce yourself to the Assembly, and to Child as well? The kiddo is very excited to know more about you."

Mr. Time believed humans should not waste time, and he especially did not want to be the reason for any wasted time, so he answered tersely: "Folks, have a good time. Don't waste time and don't sleep, ever. Don't be half dead; wake up! You don't have much time, and I know it."

It was clear Mr. Time would not say any more, so Child went back to its seat, still thinking about the nature of time.

FUTURE PREDICTION

"Let me know if you need My help predicting the future. I am the creator of everything, and also the best astrologer in the world," said God, stepping close to Mr. Future, attempting to make His presence felt at the beginning of Day Four.

"Definitely not you, but thanks for your offer, Mr. God, dude," said Mr. Future.

"I am not 'God, dude,' I am almighty God," corrected God, sounding a bit miffed at Mr. Future's casual tone.

"Okay, no offense. I will try not to use 'dude' any more. Okay? Happy now, Mr. Serious God?" said Mr. Future, smiling and pinching God's cheeks as if He were a child, which God did not like, causing Him to step back in embarrassment.

Mr. Future pointed at Mr. Marriage and said, "Before we can predict this guy's future, the basic question we should ask ourselves is, 'Historically, what has been the strongest influencing factor on him?'"

"That's easy," said Mr. Truth. "It's definitely God and His religion."

"Exactly; that's the point. We need to first understand the future of God and religion in human society in order to predict the future of Mr. Marriage. Do you get my point?" asked Mr. Future.

"Yes, of course," said Mr. Truth.

"Now, with the knowledge of Mr. Present and Mr. Past, I can

imagine Mr. Marriage in one of two possible ways in the future," said Mr. Future, as his fingers danced in the air. He was calculating variables in space on his incomprehensibly advanced virtual screen, where he ran models to predict the future.

"What are these two possibilities?" asked Mr. Truth, curious about the symbols on Mr. Future's virtual screen.

"The first," said Mr. Future, "is that things will continue in the same way they are going now, with people questioning both religion and marriage. In this possible future, society will have fewer God-believers, and even fewer marriage-lovers. Let us call this possibility 'Version One: the Usual Future.' It is an extension of a confused and conflicted present," said Mr. Future, looking at his model on the virtual screen.

Mr. Future focused on the virtual models for a moment, and then spoke again.

"The other version is a scary one. We all need to admit that however old God is, he is still a capable player and could cunningly regain his control over humans. He has done it many times before, and I am confident that he will do it again and again. With that assumption, I see another possible version of marriage in the future, where both Mr. Marriage and God will revert to their glorious state of absolute control: the kind of control one might not even imagine possible. Let us call this version of the future 'Version Two: the Godly Deadly Future,'" said Mr. Future.

"I am not cunning," said God, shaking His head in disagreement. "You might want to take those words back. I do things for the common good of the people."

"Please ignore Him, and explain the Usual Future first," requested Mr. Truth.

"You cannot disrespect Me like this, you are not even listening to Me," said God helplessly, raising His hands in disappointment.

"Please continue, Mr. Future," insisted Mr. Truth.

Mr. Marriage and the people in the Assembly looked at God in His helplessness.

Mr. Marriage laughed, and yelled at God, "Might be time to think about saving Your own ass!"

THE USUAL FUTURE AND MARRIAGE

Mr. Future began his explanation of the Usual Future by stating that people were already extremely confused about the definition, objective, and form of marriage under the rule of Mr. Present. The Usual Future would entail greater confusion about Mr. Marriage, but this confusion would lead to some positive changes in human society.

Both Mr. Marriage and God would always be in conflict with human society. They were not willing to lose control over people, and people would not stop questioning them. It would become difficult for religion to control their thoughts any longer. Mr. Future predicted a constant battle between the Marriage Police and ordinary people. Death would come to many.

Recollecting the difficulty he had had in understanding the definition of marriage on Day Three, Mr. Truth asked Mr. Future, "Can you tell me the definition of marriage in the Usual Future?"

"It will be the same as now," answered Mr. Future. "The debate regarding the definition of marriage will continue between men, women, Flexihumans, and God. Since the definition of marriage—which God says is between a man and a woman—is influenced by religion, people will continue to fight and kill, but it will gradually get better."

Mr. Future predicted that in a few nations, it would be possible to redefine marriage by making it open. Beautiful men would be able to marry men, and courageous women would be able to marry women. He predicted, looking at his model, that marriage would take on interesting new forms, and God would have a problem with these amendments to the institution.

Mr. Philosopher went through the crowd, holding and raising the hands of all the Flexihumans he could find, and sang:

"The time will come when a man will freely hold his man,

When his fear will die and his lonely eyes will not cry.

He can live, and live with him not just in heart, but under the same roof.

No need to strive; none can pull you apart, like two threads in the warp and woof.

The Future will not be dark; you will leave the world with a lovely mark.

A word of caution: try to avoid God and his religion.

He is just one, but he's already employed devils who can take everything you've done."

Mr. Truth looked at the beautiful man who had given his testimony earlier in the trial, and said, "See, your future is bright. You will be permitted to marry and do whatever you want to do. Isn't that great news?"

"Yes," said the beautiful man, smiling shyly.

THE USUAL FUTURE AND FLEXIHUMANS

As both Mr. Truth and the beautiful man started feeling a little better about the future, Mr. Future moved his eyes from his model, looked at the beautiful man, and said, "Hold on, dear, hold on." He frowned, looking worried, and continued.

"Though Flexihumans will be permitted to marry in a few nations, you will have achieved little success in your quest to be accepted by society. Many nations will permit you to marry, but you will still find it difficult to make appropriate changes with Mr. Law. You will have to fight against God to get equal rights and status in all walks of life. It will be messy, for sure."

"That's okay," said Mr. Truth. "I am happy that Flexihumans will at least be protected and recognized. At least they will be treated as fellow humans eventually."

"Yes, they will be," said Mr. Future.

He went on to explain to the Assembly that it would be true in a few nations of the world and on paper, but it would take many years to make the whole world understand and accept Flexihumans. He predicted that, interestingly, even though the Marriage Police would be responsible for their protection, there would be many cases of the Marriage Police exploiting Flexihumans, who would still be in the minority.

Mr. Truth asked impatiently, "Isn't there a better or quicker way to make everyone understand and respect individuals, regardless of whether they are Flexihumans or traditional humans? Many years from now is too long of a wait!"

"It's not possible, because religion will still be alive," responded Mr. Future.

"I see," said Mr. Truth, looking at God and shaking his head.

"However, there will be a gradual shift in the objective of marriage," said Mr. Future.

Mr. Marriage, innocently reminiscing about his past, asked from the center of the stage, "Will people ever know that I was very powerful during the rule of Mr. Past?"

"No," said Mr. Future. "They will try not to remember. People will not invite you into their lives any more. They will prefer to keep you and God at a distance. However, it will be a struggle for them, since you and God will both try to enter their lives without invitation, despite being unnecessary institutions."

Mr. Marriage sulked, folding his body and burying his head in his arms.

Mr. Truth insisted that Mr. Future explain how the objective of marriage would change in the future.

"Everything will be challenged. I mean everything. As a matter of fact, these challenges have already started in the present," said Mr. Future.

He went on to explain that the concept of husband and wife as different yet complementary would be challenged. That a child needed a mother and a father to have a normal life would be challenged. The expectation of a husband and wife becoming closer and more faithful because of children would be challenged. Marrying solely for the purpose of procreation would become outdated. Sexual fidelity would be a joke. Marriage would not be defined as though it were meant to last a lifetime.

"If it is not for a lifetime, what will it be like?" asked Mr. Truth curiously, while everyone in the Assembly muttered in surprise at what Mr. Future had said.

"I am not sure, but it might be on a contractual basis," Mr. Future responded matter-of-factly. "First, it will be for six months, then for one year, then perhaps two years, and then for five years. Marriage will become a flexible plan in the future. It will be like how we renew a driver's license. It won't be a big deal, dude," said Mr. Future, smiling casually.

"This will change the fundamental structure of society in the future. Of course it is a big deal," remarked Mr. Truth.

"Yes, of course," answered Mr. Future. "The basic building block of society will no longer be the traditional family, with a husband, a wife, and 'legitimate' children. Society will be more individualistic, with different lifestyles. Many people will prefer to live alone. People will prefer their freedom instead of the obligations that come with the institution of marriage.

"They will no longer look at sex as a divine thing that should be done with only one partner, or only after marriage. They will consider sex to be a pleasurable act with the consent of their partner, and they may have many partners. They will not believe in lifelong, permanent relationships. They will be open to the idea of leaving their partners if they are not happy. In the process, they will prefer to move in together until one of the partners loses interest in the other."

"How about their marriages?" asked God curiously, biting His nails.

Suddenly, Mr. Marriage got excited and raised his head.

"Marriage is the last thing they will think about. They will have companions, but not legal and obligatory partnerships," smiled Mr. Future.

"What will cause such a drastic change in society?" Mr. Truth asked Mr. Future.

"Less religious influence," answered Mr. Future. "In the Usual Future, people will have less fear of God. People will no longer fear social humiliation. With society moving away from the collective good to individual reasoning, the very first thing that will fall apart is people's fear of religion. Consequently, they will lose their fear of and obedience to Mr. Marriage.

"This will lead to open minds and greater acceptance of individuals with different inclinations, including Flexihumans. People will become more open to the idea of one man with multiple women, one woman with multiple men, or individual multiple marriages. The ideas of polygyny, polyandry, and polyamory will become open for debate again, and society will have the appetite to change and invite new ideas that we might not have even heard of so far."

"Will anyone marry at all?" asked Mr. Truth.

"A few will. But the idea of people marrying based on qualities of skin color, religion, wealth, or family name will be eliminated. The choice of a partner will be very personal," answered Mr. Future.

"How about children? Will parents have any say in their children's partner selection?" asked God.

"Not necessarily. There will come a time in the future when children might simply inform their parents of their choices, but parents will have no say whatsoever in their children's decisions. It's not a surprise, as one can already see this change happening now," explained Mr. Future.

"With so many Flexihumans, what about children? Who will be the dad and who will be the mom?" asked God, smiling smugly, as if He had posed an unanswerable question.

People in the Assembly were wondering why God was asking such questions, when He claimed to be all knowing of the future.

"The new concepts of two-daddy families and two-mommy families will be very common, and that answers your question," said Mr. Future.

He explained that in "Flexifamilies," love would be all over the place, and kids might call one man "Daddy" and the other man "Papa." Likewise, in a two-mommy family, one person might be called "Mommy" and the other "Mama."

"Daddy One loves Daddy Two," said Mr. Future with a whimsical smile. "I predict that it won't be uncommon to have two-daddy and two-mommy families, unlike in the present age, when families are still mostly mom-and-dad combinations. But kids grow up with equal love, even in Flexifamilies. Love matters, not gender."

Mr. Truth questioned Mr. Future about God. "What about Him? Will He be silently watching this happening, without doing anything?"

"Of course not," said Mr. Future. "He will still fight tirelessly with Mr. Law to avoid making any changes. He and the church will still not accept a man and woman as divorced, even if they are legally divorced. There will be a constant battle between God's Marriage Police and the general human population," said Mr. Future.

"Will I win?" asked God.

"You should know. Aren't you the one who says you know the future, dude?" asked Mr. Future, smiling.

"Of course I shall win, in the name of the Father," said God optimistically.

"Please shut up," said Mr. Truth, and asked Mr. Future, "What will happen, what do you see?"

"Sorry," said Mr. Future. "I cannot see that far, but it will be a long, long battle for many years, for sure."

The Usual Future and the Next Level:
HUMAN-ANIMAL MARRIAGE

The Usual Future, with people having the freedom to choose how they lived, sounded horrific to God's ears.

Mr. Marriage had been silently listening to Mr. Future's predictions, not misbehaving like usual. Now, he asked Mr. Future, "If you let a man marry another man, and define marriage based on love, what about humans who love animals? Can they also marry them in the future?"

"Yes, dude," said Mr. Future. "Moving from interracial to interspecies marriage will be the next thing. It is not a certainty, but the possibility of people marrying across species is strong, I can say that," said Mr. Future.

When one rule is broken, then the second rule certainly will be, wrote Mr. Philosopher.

"Blasphemous!" said God. "In the name of the Father, don't say that man will marry animals! Man is special; he is not another animal. I created him with My hands."

"It's unfortunate, but Your precious man is just an animal, belonging to the class Mammalia. That's the truth, like it or not," said Mr. Truth.

The people sitting in the Assembly were angry at Mr. Truth's statement. They had always thought God's own hands had specially created them. They did not like the idea of being equal to other life forms. They also thought that Earth had been created by God as a special gift for them, and that the sun shone during the day and the moon shone at night because it suited humanity's lifestyle.

"Mr. Truth, we need to stop here. Declaring that humans are animals will have dire consequences on their behavior. Be aware of that," God warned him.

"Dire consequences? Like what?" asked Mr. Truth.

"Today, humans think they are special, that they are better than animals. If they all listened to their animal insides, they would start exhibiting animal behavior, which might not be good for collective human society," said God.

"Even today, humans exhibit a lot of animal behavior, don't they?" countered Mr. Truth. "The one thing the human animal has more of than all other species is intelligence. As long as humans have this quality, they will continue to be at the top of the animal kingdom. You mustn't worry."

"But not everyone is intelligent," God argued. "Some people show their true selves like animals do. If they receive proven confirmation of being animals, how can we stop them from committing animal acts? Men will start justifying their sexual behavior by claiming it is normal animal behavior."

God was getting more and more agitated, His voice growing

louder with each word. "We won't be able to stop it! Where will we stop? It's an ugly future to imagine men committing non-reproductive sexual behaviors!" He finished on a scream.

"What do those behaviors include?" asked Child innocently.

"To begin with, oral sex is exhibited in wolves, goats, and sheep. Can you imagine men doing it? Sex involving juveniles, which is common in chimpanzees. Can you imagine an elderly man mounting the back of a young girl?" said God, observing that the people in the gallery were consuming this information with a lot of interest.

He started walking towards Child and raised His voice, addressing the Assembly like a preacher addressing a congregation.

"How about necrophilia, where an animal engages in a sexual act with the dead? This happens with birds and frogs. Can you imagine a man having a sexual engagement with a dead woman's body? It's not a nice image. We have to have rules, and we do have rules—right here in *The H Book*," He finished angrily.

"Rules are the domain of Mr. Law," said Mr. Truth, noting that Child and some of the people in the Assembly looked like they might believe what God had said. "It is not the role of religion to make such rules, because there are different versions of religious books and different books might have different rules."

"Hold on, dudes," said Mr. Future. "You guys have certainly taken the matter of someone marrying an animal to a totally different level. I was talking about someone legally linked to his dearly beloved pet; I was not talking about dirty sex with another animal," said Mr. Future.

"Isn't this typical of You, God?" said Mr. Truth. "Trying to portray a dark, ugly image to justify Your system? You've proven it again. You cannot manufacture horror in people, and then address the same horror with Your preaching."

Child was scared of the image God had described of Mr. Man aggressively violating the dead body of a woman. He looked at Mr. Man fearfully.

"Oh, Child, don't you get scared," said God, softly stroking Child's hair. "I am here and I will protect you, in the name of the Father," said God, hugging Child too tightly and rubbing its back too hard. Child was not comfortable with God's hug.

"Just leave Child alone," said Mr. Future. "It should know the truth; it needs to know reality in order to decide its future."

Mr. Truth slowly pulled Child from God's arms.

"At what cost?" asked God.

"At the cost of Child losing innocence but gaining knowledge. However, I request that you stop scaring children," replied Mr. Truth, helping Child back to its judge's seat. "Now, Mr. Future, do you have anything more to say about the Usual Future?"

Mr. Future cleared his throat and smiled, easily commanding the attention of the Assembly again.

"In summary," he began, "the Usual Future will be colorful; it will unite the colors of the human race. People will be bored with marrying within the same caste, community, skin color, and religion; they will start enjoying relationships with people from other communities. The length of most marriages will not be more than two to three years, since people will realize that there is no afterlife and science will have proven that there are no souls or ghosts.

"People will start using their lives preciously. They will no longer believe in sacrifices and obligations. A few of them will have great two- or three-year marriages, if they ever marry, then move on to the next phase of life with a new partner. Divorce will be easy, and there will be a debate about getting rid of the concept of alimony, since men and women will be socially and economically equal." Mr. Future looked pleased with his description.

Mr. Truth had filled a lot of pages in his notebook. "Thank you, Mr. Future," he said. "Now, would you please explain the second possible version of the future?"

The Godly Deadly Future:
MARRIAGE AND THE REGAINING OF CONTROL

Mr. Future took some time to create another model on his screen.

"As we have already seen," he said, "in the present, with the rise of gender equality, love-based marriages, and human curiosity, Mr. Marriage and God are gradually losing control over humanity. This will continue in the Godly Deadly Future as well as the Usual Future. People will start seeing marriage as a social obligation and doubting its worth. They will start living freely, without asking permission from Mr. Marriage or Mr. Law to love or live with someone. This disobedience will annoy both God and Mr. Marriage. God knows this disobedience will put an end to the era of his control over men and women, and he will not want to let that happen."

"But what can He do?" asked Mr. Truth.

"Both Mr. Marriage and God will approach Mr. Law," said Mr. Future. "The rulers of all the nations will make a pact. Since the rulers are all God-loving, they are supposed to be God-abiding as well. God will influence the rulers and Mr. Law, and will succeed in getting *The H Book* included in every national constitution. He will also get permission to let the Marriage Police carry out punishments in all nations, and they will be above national laws and law enforcement bodies."

Mr. Philosopher added, "It's rare to find a leader of a nation who is not a God-lover or a marriage-believer. It always helps for a leader to be able to relate to the common people. This is how a leader is born out of the unintelligent majority."

Mr. Future continued his prediction. "With the collusion of national rulers, changes will be made not only to the law, but to education. People will be indoctrinated with God's agenda. The concept of love for other people will be replaced by the concept of duty to God and Mr. Marriage. The Marriage Police will be instructed to kill people in the streets at their discretion if they find any citizens breaking the laws of *The H Book*, the Commandments, or the new rules."

"Will public execution for violation of the rules be the only possible punishment?" asked Mr. Truth.

"A few cases may be sent to the Island in order to demonstrate the nature of punishment to the general public. But most of them will be punished immediately," said Mr. Future.

"What is the Island?"

"The Island is a place where sinners will be punished," said Mr. Future. "I'll tell you more about the Island in a few minutes."

"What about us?" asked one of the Flexihumans.

"Bad news for you guys in the Godly Deadly Future," said Mr. Future. "In a matter of fifty years, you will all be dead, considered an extinct species. People will have discovered a technology to identify the sexual inclinations of a child at birth, and because it is against God and his *H Book*, children with same-sex inclinations will be killed at birth."

"Bad news for you as well," said Mr. Future to Mr. Philosopher. "Philosophizing will be an illegal act. There will be no philosophers left alive in the Godly Deadly Future. All books except *The H Book* will be burned, and people will not be permitted to write at all."

"Death sounds sweeter than living in the Godly Deadly Future," said Mr. Philosopher.

Mr. Future continued. "In just a few years, humans will go back to living in fear of Mr. Marriage, God, and Mr. Law. They will not have any choice but to accept the law of the land, which will include religion. People will be expected to perform even their professional activities as dictated by God and Mr. Marriage.

"Anything that does not advance the greater good of society in the name of duty and the collective brotherhood will be considered sinful. And even though I will be the official ruler of the time, my title will be only a formality; I will not be able to do anything. God and Mr. Marriage will become the real rulers of the future."

GODLY DEADLY MARRIAGE AND THE
NEW ANTHEM

"Marriage will again become the central theme of everyone's life," Mr. Future went on. He spoke as calmly as always. "Mr. Marriage and God will be comfortable in their existence, power, and absolute authority over society," he added.

Hearing this, God smiled, but Mr. Marriage was still lost in thought, looking disturbed, as if he did not want the Godly Deadly Future to happen.

Mr. Future continued talking, consulting his virtual model.

"In the Godly Deadly Future, in all nations there will be statues of both God and Mr. Marriage in every school, university, assembly, and public place. There will be a combined photo of God and Mr. Marriage in every house, in every advertisement, in every printed book, and on every currency note and coin. Coins and bills will have God on one side and Mr. Marriage on the other."

"This is worse than a totalitarian state," commented Mr. Truth.

"True," agreed Mr. Future, still in his same mild, unconcerned tone. "In any location, from any angle, one will always be able to see representations of God and Mr. Marriage. Religious songs and hymns to the goodness of Mr. Marriage will be played around the clock in all streets, workplaces, and even private houses. Even in restrooms, both public and private, people will not be able to escape. Every moment of a person's existence will include God and Mr. Marriage."

217

"But why? What is the point of all that?" asked Mr. Truth.

"The point is to instill the concepts of God and marriage into human life so deeply that they appear to be natural and innate," answered Mr. Future.

"How about love?" asked Mr. Truth.

"In the Godly Deadly Future, where duty rules, love will not be a subject that is entertained or taken seriously," answered Mr. Future matter-of-factly.

"Love will be a dead concept, and affection an outdated one. The concept of love will be used only in marketing and sales as part of God's business. But people will not experience love any more. Men will no longer make love; they will only have hard, mechanical sex. They will be unaware of the concept of orgasm. Instead, they will regularly inject themselves with a colorless fluid called 'high lie,' which will be provided in all public places; it will get them high and cause them to ejaculate without a real orgasm. The natural orgasm will become a concept of the past.

"People will only have the duty to make kids, not to love them. Affection will be considered an inferior attribute only found in animals and birds. Humans will claim their superiority as they watch animals in zoos, like wolves or gibbons, rub each other's cheeks and necks, or birds touching and licking each other's beaks. These gestures will be considered entertainment, since humans will not exhibit such behaviors at all. Anything done in the name of pleasure will qualify as 'unproductive,' and will be completely forbidden in the Godly Deadly Future," he finished.

The people in the Assembly were nervous now.

Before anyone could ask more about love, Mr. Future continued: "All nations will share a common World Anthem, in addition to their individual national anthems. The World Anthem will be printed in all books, and everyone will be legally required to know the Anthem. The Marriage Police will have the authority to ask anyone, randomly, to sing the Anthem. Failure to sing the Anthem will result in the Marriage Police cutting out the person's tongue. Officers of the Marriage Police will be promoted based on the number of tongues they cut out each day.

"The World Anthem will go like this:

'God save the world!

God save our fallacious lives!

Long live our noble Marriage!

God save our world!

Send us prosperity,

Happy and wondrous,

Long to rule over us,

God save our world!

O Marriage and God arise!

Scatter our reason,

Make us unintelligent,

Confound our rationality,

Frustrate any intelligent thoughts!

On you both our hope we fix,

God save our world!'

"All countries will sing the same Anthem in the name of God and Mr. Marriage. People will gradually start swearing on marriage; for example, 'I swear on dear Mr. Marriage that I did not do...' in their daily speech. There will be temples to Mr. Marriage with idols of him. People will worship out of fear and duty, not love," Mr. Future concluded.

"Will I live all my life in fear and obedience, or will I have any kind of amusement in the Godly Deadly future?" asked Mr. Man.

"Yes, you'll have 'fun' in the Men's Park," said Mr. Future.

THE GODLY DEADLY FUTURE
AND THE MEN'S PARK

Mr. Future spun his model faster. "The Men's Park is the place where sinners will be forced to demonstrate what happens to people who don't follow the rules, especially people who make the mistake of loving another person," explained Mr. Future.

Mr. Man looked interested but apprehensive.

"In the Men's Park, sinners will entertain the rest of the world by demonstrating their sins. They will be required to put on a show to convey a strong message about goodness and the forgiving nature of God and Mr. Marriage," explained Mr. Future. "Men and women who have sinned will be placed in the Men's Park, which will be located alongside the Zoo Park. The Men's Park will attract more visitors and make more money. Humans will be put alongside the animals to exhibit their sinful affectionate behavior."

"This just does not seem practical," said Mr. Truth. "I cannot even imagine humans in cages like animals, demonstrating lovemaking. How is this possible? Please explain."

"Yes, it's inhuman," answered Mr. Future. "But that's not even the worst of it. Men and women will be medically aroused, since their punishment will entail continuously exhibiting their sinful behavior, twenty-four-seven, throughout the year, for twenty-five years. At the beginning of the public show, these men and women will be required to demonstrate their passionate and sinful love for each other while naked, stating that they used to believe there was true love beyond duty, affection beyond sex, and life beyond marriage. At the end of the show, they will be forced to confess that all the passion, love, and life beyond marriage they used to believe in was a lie, and they will state that they should have just followed their sense of duty, not their minds and hearts. They will also confess their guilt, and, finally, thank God and Mr. Marriage for forgiving them, and for sending them to the Island."

"Please tell us more about what will happen on this Island," requested Mr. Truth, intrigued.

WHAT HAPPENS ON THE ISLAND REMAINS

ON THE ISLAND

Mr. Future launched into an explanation of the elaborate hierarchy of punishments that would be meted out on the Island, consulting his virtual model frequently.

He told the Assembly that punishments on the Island would fall into three categories: the Preliminary Round, the Entertainment Round, and the Final Round. The Preliminary Round would last one week, the Entertainment Round three hundred and sixty days, and the Final Round ninety days.

During the Preliminary Round, the Marriage Police would take sinners to the Island, which would not be located on any maps, in order to prevent ordinary people from finding it. Upon reaching the Island, the sinners' clothes would be taken away; they would remain naked for the rest of their stay. Then they would be taken into an investigation chamber, where they would be interrogated about whether they had ever kissed someone they loved, or had feelings for anyone. It would not be possible for the prisoners to lie, because the Internet Conglomeration would be able to instantly provide evidence from surveillance videos.

When sinners inevitably answered yes to the first question, their mouths would be sliced open to the ears, and acid applied to the cuts to cause more pain. Their mouths would then be stapled back up before they moved on to the next round of questions. The Marriage Police would clearly instruct the sinners to be silent, telling them that if they screamed or showed pain at all, the Marriage Police would rip their mouths open further, stapling more and more, until the sinners maintained their silence. This punishment would be the same for both genders.

In the Entertainment Round, the sinners would be taken to an open field along with all the other sinners, where the authorities would be watching. Couples guilty of the sin of love would be forced to demonstrate their love for each other openly in the field. This demonstration would always include sex. Couples would be forced to demonstrate every act of love they had ever committed, without exception, as the Internet Conglomeration would have evidence of all the acts previously committed.

The crowd would scream and catcall instructions to the lovers: "Bite lips! Pinch nipples! Eat pussy!"

After their public acts of love, the sinful man would be forced to select three men, and the sinful woman would be forced to select three women, from among the other prisoners. The sinful man would be forced to watch the three men he had selected rape the sinful woman, and likewise, the sinful woman would be forced to watch the three women she had selected rape the sinful man. This part of the punishment would be designed to make the sinful man insensitive toward the sinful woman, and vice versa.

During the rapes, the authorities would keep track of who spent the most time humping, going wild and counting, "One, two, three, four..." The rapist with the highest count would receive hearty congratulations. The Entertainment Round would continue every day for three hundred and sixty days, provided the sinners remained alive. No rule would stipulate that death should stop the entertainment, as prisoners on the Island could then demonstrate the sin of having sex with dead bodies.

At this point in Mr. Future's description, the people in the Assembly were wide-eyed with horror, and some had begun crying out for him to stop. But Mr. Future continued as if he couldn't hear them. He was convinced it was important for people to see the whole picture of the Godly Deadly Future.

In the Final Round, as Mr. Future described it, both the sinful man and the sinful woman would be treated well, given the best food and a clean shelter for thirty days. They would be sequestered from the other prisoners. On the thirtieth day, when the sinful man and woman sat at the dining table together, the authorities would observe whether they picked up a knife or a fork first. This would be how the authorities decided whether to use a knife or a fork in their final round of punishment. It would be considered lucky to be punished with the knife, even though the knives would be blunt and rusted.

MARRIAGELESS

After their thirtieth dinner together, the sinful man and woman would be tied to a cold iron bar next to each other. The knife or fork from dinner would then be used to cut off the man's cock, with the procedure taking a minimum of ninety minutes. After a break of thirty minutes, his balls would also be freed from his body. This would take a minimum of sixty minutes.

The sinful woman's breasts would be cut off, which would take two hours, and then her vagina would be stitched up, which would take thirty minutes. Immediately, the six other prisoners who had been forced to rape the sinful man and woman during the previous round would be called back and ordered to rape them again. Most of the time, both the sinful man and woman would die from blood loss.

The few who survived the amputations and the rapes would be operated upon, artificial cocks stitched onto the men and artificial breasts on the women. They would be given artificial tongues. They would live for sixty more days on the Island, reading *The H Book* and chanting, "*Long live Mr. Marriage and God! Never love anyone! Live dutifully!*" a million times a day, before being released from the Island to the Men's Park.

Only one out of every thousand prisoners would survive, but those who did would likely die of sexually transmitted diseases or the physical and psychological wounds caused by the torture they had endured. Mr. Law would not address these violations of human rights, in order to maintain fear of the Island in the hearts and minds of the people.

Mr. Truth was shocked for the first time in the course of the trial, imagining the kind of blood and horror that might become reality in the Godly Deadly Future. He blacked out momentarily, then raised his hands, signaling to Mr. Future to stop talking. Mr.

Truth slowly looked around to see the millions of faces of men and women in the gallery, and finally turned back to face Child, who looked even more terrified than before. Mr. Truth forced a smile to comfort Child, then moved the proceedings along.

THE GODLY DEADLY FUTURE
AND CHILDREN

"What about kids in the Godly Deadly Future?" asked Mr. Truth. "How will they be born without a man loving a woman? Just pure hard sex?"

"Not really. Not even that," answered Mr. Future.

He explained that in both versions of the future, natural birth would be a rare incident in society, and when it happened—usually only in the case of a few housemaids—it would be a newsworthy event, appearing on all channels in the *Joke of the Day* section.

"Most men and women," Mr. Future went on, "will see natural birth as an uncontrolled behavior and a waste of time and energy, distracting from more productive work. Children will most commonly be born through technology, with subtle human assistance and help. People will be able to genetically customize their kids, choosing from various options. Some of these options will be: skin color and tone, height, hair type, eye shape, and nose shape.

"Then the Child Factory will work up a proof of concept, and once the prototype of the kid is ready, the customer will approve it and place the order. The child will be assembled by the Smiley Clouds, using the advanced techniques of the new Internet Conglomeration 2.1, then gestated in mini-balloons within the clouds.

"The child will be delivered within twenty-four hours of an order being placed. In the end, the family photo will be perfect, with all members of the family smiling smiles of equal length. The photo will be all that matters," said Mr. Future in conclusion.

"This is insane," remarked Mr. Truth, while the Assembly looked terrified of the future they were hearing described.

"How will God and Mr. Marriage have so much control?" asked Mr. Truth. "Will they use the Eye-Phones?"

"Yes, but in a quite advanced mode, dude," answered Mr. Future. "In the Godly Deadly Future, every human will be born with an embedded tool set. This tool set will include the Eye-Phone, which will be like an organ on the back of the hand. The organic Eye-Phones will be the single point of contact for every individual. People will start to believe Eye-Phones are natural parts of the body like eyes, hands, or legs.

"With the help of the Eye-Phones, Mr. Marriage and God will be able to monitor everyone's movements, thought processes, actions, and choices. If they find any subversive ideas in a person's mind, the Marriage Police will be notified immediately and the person will either be killed or taken to the Island.

"Given the success of current research about organic Eye-Phones in Area 2.51, there will be ongoing research into methods of completely manipulating the thoughts and choices of humans right from the time of birth, instead of through monitoring and punishing. That research will go on for many centuries, however, since the human mind will not be easy to comprehend, even with the help of advanced Area 2.51 research and development."

"Will anything be like the life people have in the present?" asked Mr. Truth.

"Some of it," answered Mr. Future. "People will go to school at the same age. All schools will have the same syllabus and teaching techniques. The motto in all schools will be, '*One day, you will be married and God will bless you.*' Kids will grow up thinking that they must marry, and there will be no one who thinks differently.

"In the immediate Godly Deadly Future, everyone will have to go to war. People will not fight for countries any more; they will fight in the name of faith against people who don't believe in marriage. But in the later stages of Godly Deadly Future, with the help of the advanced version of the Internet Conglomeration 2.1, all humans will be obedient, and these wars will not happen.

"All kids will grow up with a great deal of curiosity and anxiety about reaching the life goal of marriage. They will also be taught about the Island, and once a year, they will be taken to the Men's Park to see the consequences of not being obedient. And that concludes my description of the Godly Deadly Future," said Mr. Future, closing the models on his virtual screens.

Mr. Truth had stopped taking notes in his case file, because he himself could not imagine the Godly Deadly Future. Mr. Marriage was still thinking, appearing unusually introspective. God was the only one on the stage who looked content.

Mr. Truth ended the day by declaring, "This is the end of Day Four. Have fun for the rest of the evening. See you all tomorrow, for Judgment Day."

The entertainers ran onto the stage, but the people in the Assembly were not in any mood for entertainment. They were thinking and fearing—thinking of the possible futures and fearing the next day's judgment. They had certainly heard a lot on Day Four, and knew that Judgment Day would be a momentous day.

MARRIAGELESS

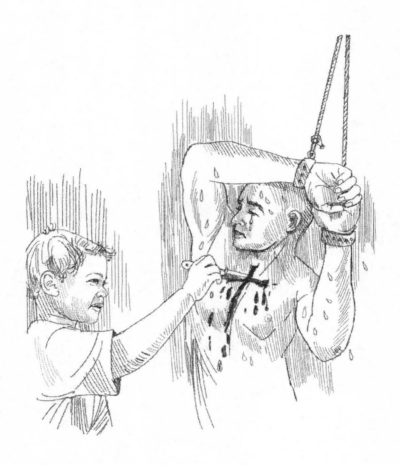

7

THE END

THE JUDGMENT, THE ANSWER, AND THE BOOK

JUDGMENT DAY

It was the fifth and last day of the Assembly: Judgment Day. Even in the morning hours, the sky was covered with thick gray clouds. There was little trace of sun, and the wind was slowly blowing with a low whistle, as if screaming devils were hidden in the thick gray.

While Mr. Philosopher and Mr. Truth looked at the people in the Assembly, Mr. Philosopher said, "After today, the people will miss the arguments. We all know that arguments make up life while judgment is the end of everything, just as the journey is life while the destination is the end of the road. But people always run towards their goals, saving the beauty to cherish only when they reach the finish line. They don't realize that standing at the goal, all you get is a vacuum."

MARRIAGELESS

Mr. Philosopher cleared his throat and sang, looking at Mr. Man and Mrs. Woman, who anxiously awaited the start of the proceedings.

"The 'beginning of the end' marks the end of few beginnings.

Pain ends with pleasure and pleasure ends with pain.

In this cycle of endings and beginnings, we all dance in the rain of time.

This rain will never stop; your dance will stop, but not this rain.

At times, time itself is a problem and a solution.

But everything ends, including your dear son; all that you've won and every action of your life will be undone.

Your life is just a spray of a few images in color in different expressions across different times.

Marriage will end, God will also bend, but Man will invent his new depression.

Nothing can help him, when he knows: his life has no purpose but to question.

And he knows that questions can only lead to questions and questions, but that's his only known profession.

God was the next to take the stage. He stood gracefully in one corner, deep in thought.

Mr. Present and Mr. Past were next to take the stage, and they sat in their respective seats.

Mr. Marriage was dragged onto the center of the stage by security.

Mr. Future and Child entered the scene last, along with Old Man, and for some reason, they were nodding in agreement as Old Man explained something to both of them.

Mr. Truth stopped in the center of the stage. "Let us begin. May I request the revered judges Future and Child come to the front and give their verdict, please," said Mr. Truth.

"Hold on, My son; hold that thought," said God, walking towards the center of the stage where Mr. Truth stood. "You seem to be in a real hurry. Is Judgment Day really required? Can we not leave things the way they are, and end the proceedings now?"

Mr. Truth was not surprised to hear what God said; he had expected some attempt from Him to stop the proceedings of Judgment Day.

"No. What do You mean by 'leave things the way they are'? We did all this hard work for the last four days to reach this place of judgment. This is definitely needed, without any doubt," answered Mr. Truth.

God knew Mr. Truth would not agree easily.

"I understand," He said. "We've all worked hard. More than anyone, I did the work of building the Great Assembly, coordinating with all the people, and organizing the event. We've made great progress, indeed. We've made people aware of the present, past, and possible futures. I think our mission has been accomplished. We can end this case here with a sweet goodbye note to all the participants, who have come a long way from many different nations. I am sure they must be tired by now. Let us kiss them sweet goodbye, in the name of the Father," persisted God.

"I repeat: Judgment Day is required. It is the objective of the Great Assembly. To begin with, wasn't it You who invented the concept of judging every man and woman?" asked Mr. Truth.

"Yes, I did, but I judge in the name of the Father, not based on human testimony or human laws," said God.

"Here, we will judge in the name of truth and reason," said Mr. Truth.

For the sake of gathering more information, Mr. Truth inquired about God's Judgment Day. "I am incapable of death, so I will never experience your Judgment Day," he said to God.

"You need to tell me about it. Do you have an Assembly like this in Your kingdom? Do You have this kind of seating arrangement? Do You have judges and mediators discussing the merits of the case, asking questions of the offender, and interviewing the witnesses?" asked Mr. Truth.

"Not exactly," replied God. "On My Judgment Day, I sit on the white throne. On the floor, one can see millions of human heads. These are from the sinners who have been beheaded for not worshipping Me, or for worshipping Me in a way other than *The H Book* prescribes. They did not follow the marriage rules as I recommended. The dead stand in a never-ending line in the sky and bow in front of My throne out of respect for Me. They wait for their turn to be judged. I command one of my angels to read *The Book of Human Life* and judge the dead based on the good and bad that is written in the book," God explained proudly.

"So, it is very similar. We have come a long way in recreating everything God created, and in a better way," said Mr. Truth.

God ignored him, and went on to explain His method of judgment, obviously excited by the opportunity to describe His acts of power. "If a person has more negatives than positives, I will order that they be stripped naked and painted with oils before being pierced through the neck with a stake and roasted over the ocean of fire. If a person's name is missing from *The Book of Human Life*, regardless of whether they are good or bad, they will be thrown in the same ocean of fire."

"How do you determine positives and negatives?" asked Mr. Truth.

"It's simple. People should worship Me, and Me alone. Second, they should follow all the Commandments and other rules of marriage as I prescribe. It's just that simple. If they do, they will have positives in *The Book of Human Life* and I will give them a pass to Heaven," God explained.

"What if they have not worshipped You, but were good to their fellow humans and were truthful and honest all their lives? What if they were never married, but they were charitable people?" asked Mr. Truth.

"It does not matter," said God. "There is only one exception to the 'compulsory marriage' rule: men who opt not to marry must dedicate their entire lives to preaching *The H Book* all over the world, and celebrate celibacy all their lives. Such a man's life's objectives must be God and *The H Book*. By doing that, a man who does not marry can escape Hell."

"Thank you for that information. Now, let us get back to our case. We will judge Mr. Marriage today. I repeat, we will have Judgment Day," said Mr. Truth.

Completely irritated with the exchange between God and Mr. Truth, Mr. Marriage screamed, "What the fuck is going on here? Are you guys going to talk some shit nonsense related to God and His screwed up judgment, or fucking decide my fate, here?

"I have been hungry, tired, and dirty for the last four days. Just decide. Hurry up!" shouted Mr. Marriage, in his usual coarse style.

IT'S DEATH. BLOOD HAS TO BE RED AND FED

Mr. Truth requested that both Mr. Future and Child take the stage and let all those gathered know if they had arrived at a decision. If so, he asked them to make their decision public.

Child jumped from its chair and ran to the center of the stage. It unfolded a verdict form and read out loud to the Assembly: "We have reached a verdict: death to Mr. Marriage."

"What?" said God, surprised at the way Child had pronounced the verdict.

Mr. Marriage did not even look at Child. He heard the verdict and remained lying on the stage. He was shocked, completely unmoving. The Assembly was silent. They did not know how to react to a death sentence. They were completely surprised. Moreover, they did not expect an innocent Child could cast a fatal verdict with such ease.

Mrs. Woman welcomed the decision, saying with a smile, "Thank you, Child. You are young, but you are very smart. I love you."

Mr. Philosopher wrote: *Most of the time, sadness results from losing something or someone you have gotten used to, not necessarily someone or something you love. It is valuable to make new mistakes, and keep learning new lessons until life is over. There are still many lessons to learn and sins to taste.*

"Security, take Mr. Marriage away and kill him. Make it quick," said Child, running happily back to its chair.

"Wait, this is blasphemous! I cannot let this happen. Listen to Me, My dear Child! We can end this session for today and we can resume tomorrow and decide the judgment. There is absolutely no rush to decide and execute today. Mr. Marriage has been here for the longest time; let us discuss more! In the name of the Father, please be a little patient!" pleaded God.

"No. We don't want to take any more time. It's already been delayed enough. Mr. Marriage needs to be taken out of our society," said Child, now comfortably sitting in its chair.

"Based on Mr. Past's points, Mr. Present's performance, and Mr. Future's possibilities, we have determined that we need to get rid of him. He has already become a questionable, misunderstood, unnecessary institution. Keeping him alive for even one more day will make people more confused and miserable."

"So, you want him killed right now?" asked God, still disbelieving what He was hearing.

"Yes, you've heard it right, we want him killed right now," answered Child.

"And then what will happen? How do you justify your verdict? What good will it do society? There are many answers I need to know," said God.

"Of course; these are all valid questions. I will talk about all the subjects you have raised with the humans after your execution," said Child.

"You mean Mr. Marriage's execution, right?" asked God nervously.

"No, you heard me correctly, *your* execution. You need to die as well. God must die," Child stated without mercy.

The Assembly fell silent. People stared in utter shock at Child's pronouncement.

"Did you say that I will be executed? You mean to execute the almighty God, the creator of this mother Earth, by the grace of the Father?" asked God, smiling. He still did not believe the verdict.

"Yes, I am sorry, but you need to die as well. God must die." said Child.

"This is My world, My people, My Assembly, My rules. I decide life and death, not you. In the name of My fucking Father, you cannot kill Me! How can a child kill its father?" shouted God angrily.

"Of course, as you are God, we can only make a human attempt to kill you, to test the real God in you," said Child. "If we fail, then you will certainly live."

"Blasphemous, blasphemous! If I die, Earth will burst into a thousand pieces, rains will fall for a thousand years, volcanoes will erupt until every living thing is dead, floods will rage until all visible land disappears!" screamed God.

"Let us put that to the test. We will try to execute you and string you up. Please bless us, God, so that we may be victorious," said Child, smiling.

"Child, enough. I am done with the session for today. I am leaving right now," said God. He began walking off the stage, towards the exit of the Assembly.

"Security, please chain God and make him sit with Mr. Marriage in the center of the stage," ordered Child.

Security rushed to the stage and held God's hands tightly. They chained His legs and tied His hair as God screamed out loud like a little child.

Even Mr. Truth was not expecting this verdict of God. He hurriedly went to Child and asked, "Are you sure about what you are doing?"

"Yes, I am. This is part of our judgment. Mr. Future and I have already thought about it," said Child.

God, on the other hand, still could not believe this turn of events. He started sweating, and shouted hysterically, "In the name of the Father, you cannot do this! Child, you cannot arrest Me! You cannot do this! Every child will die if you do this! Stop this blasphemous act!"

"Please stuff that shoe in God's mouth so he does not shout any more. Use the iron crook around his neck to control him," Child ordered the security officers.

"Now, wet the heads of both God and Mr. Marriage, and shave off their hair. Also, shave off God's beard and ugly mustache. Uncle God, please be silent, or else I will be forced to order thirty-nine lashes on your ass. Shut up, please."

Mr. Truth, who was still standing near Child, said, "To be fair to God, this is not a case against Him; it is a case against Mr. Marriage. If we need to punish God, we will need to discuss His case later, in a separate hearing."

"No, Mr. Truth. Mr. Marriage cannot be separated from faith and religion. Trust me, I have discussed this at length with Mr. Future. We have tried to find a perfect solution, and for a better future, we need to do this. We need to get rid of both parasites at the same time. We all know that we will never win a case against God. We all know that. We just need to kill him, without giving him a chance to play his tricks," said Child.

"Why treat God so brutally? I thought every child, if not loved

237

God, at least feared Him," asked Mr. Truth.

"Yes, you are right. I have always been afraid of God; I have never loved him. You should be familiar by now with the brutality committed in the name of faith and religion. In contrast, hanging this one God does not even balance out the millions of other deaths he has caused," said Child.

A group of men started screaming, "Save God, Kill Mr. Future! God will save us! Trust in the Lord and do not lean on your own understanding!"

"Dudes, hold on. Let me make clarify. Stop shouting," said Mr. Future.

"We want polls! We want to know what public opinion says!" screamed the men.

"You mean common rule or your stupid democracy? I love that foolish thought. We don't believe in common rule while judging. We believe in right and wrong, good and bad. If anyone is expecting a poll to decide judgment, then you are mistaken, dudes. More importantly, if anyone thinks the judgment is not fair, I am happy to help them join God," said Mr. Future, pausing dramatically.

"Who wants to join God, in the name of his Father?" he asked.

No one responded. The screaming had stopped completely.

DEATH EXPLAINED

Mr. Truth requested that Mr. Future pronounce the complete judgment for the Assembly.

Mr. Future stepped in front of everyone and started reading aloud from the document he and Child had drafted.

"God and Mr. Marriage are pronounced guilty. Mr. Marriage is convicted of using the institution of marriage to become rich and influential, lying to humanity by conspiring with God and JC, aiding God in raping millions of women, and helping him control human society using religion and marriage.

"God is also convicted of lying to humanity, killing millions of men and women in the name of faith, raping women using *The H Book* and the Commandments as justification, dividing societies in the name of religion, and starting most of the wars that have ever happened. Both of them are sentenced to death. Mr. Marriage will be given a choice of his preferred method of death, but God will be wounded and then strung up until he dies.

"Mr. Past is also convicted of following God's scriptures and committing countless crimes instead of caring for the men and women of his time, but death is not his punishment. He will be left in the forest with no human contact until the end of his life.

"Mr. Man is warned very strictly not to repeat the mistakes of his past, when he used Mr. Marriage and God to his advantage. Mrs. Woman is recognized for her role in Mr. Present's rule, and she will be given more opportunities in the future.

"We offer a special thanks to Old Man, who stood as witness to the crimes of marriage in the past. Finally, the Marriage Police will be shut down, effective immediately."

Mr. Future explained his and Child's reasoning further.

"Mr. Marriage started off well, as a protector of Woman and Child, but was later corrupted in the name of money and power. His biggest crime was his alliance with God, when he conspired against the good of society. Mr. Marriage has been responsible for a lot of death and humiliation, especially for millions of women. He has taken away the basic freedom of choice from women. Marriage has become the most confused subject in human life in the present. Society is divided on the definition and purpose of marriage.

"Additionally, the two predicted versions of the future are not encouraging reasons to keep Mr. Marriage alive. The Godly Deadly Future could be real. We did deliberate about taking a chance on keeping Mr. Marriage around in case the Usual Future comes to pass, but even in that case, getting rid of Mr. Marriage and God will certainly make human society better, instead of worse."

"Okay, but what will replace marriage?" asked Mr. Truth.

"I am not sure if there is a need for any replacement," said Child. "People will now start to believe in love, instead of family. They will have more love to share with people around them. If this love needs a definition, the individuals should be able to define it in their own personal ways. But a society or a legal body has no role to play in what happens in people's lives. Mr. Law and the state should have no business in people's personal lives."

"Okay, I get that. Mr. Marriage needs to go. But what did God do? Why are you killing Him, as well?" asked Mr. Man, sounding concerned.

"Based on the testimony from Mr. Past and what we've witnessed in the present, we made this judgment. The confusion about marriage and the crimes committed against women under Mr. Past's rule are also attributed to religion and God. Indeed, not all of these crimes were made possible by God. We, the judges, agree that in the past there were times when power and money were responsible. But for a few hundred years, it was religion that defined marriage in human society. Religion is responsible for a lot of blood spilled upon the Earth. We have to cleanse the same Earth with God's blood. Timing-wise, it helps to kill them simultaneously, so that human society can start fresh," explained Child.

"You might want to tell the Assembly more about God from the beginning," said Old Man to Child.

"Yes," said Child. "Moreover, God has always been sinning, right from the beginning. Before we got onto the stage this morning, we were informed by Old Man about what happened in the garden. We learned earlier in this trial that God raped and abused the first woman created by the Father, but I need to let everyone know that God killed his own Father, as well."

The people in the Assembly were shocked and unable to respond. They just sat, not uttering a word, even to their neighbors.

"But why would He do that?" asked Mr. Truth.

"Because God wanted to kiss his Father and sleep with Him, and Father refused his advances. Hence, God thought it would be better to get rid of his Father, who knew God's inclinations. God was also was afraid that his Father might find out from His favorite serpent what God had done to the first woman."

"So, is God bisexual, like Mr. Free?" asked Mr. Truth, confused.

"It does not matter now," said Child.

EXECUTION

The stage was set to execute Mr. Marriage first, and God next. Mr. Marriage and God were made to sit together.

God still could not speak.

Mr. Marriage could, but had not uttered a word, questioned a thing, or moved an inch from the time Child had pronounced the verdict; he was just introspectively staring at the floor of the stage.

Several of the large security officers poured water on both criminals' heads, and quickly shaved them.

"Any last wishes, Mr. Marriage? More importantly, do you want to say anything in your defense?" asked Mr. Truth.

"None, Mr. Truth, but thanks," said Mr. Marriage. He was courteous, for a change.

"Do not let him suffer. Mr. Marriage deserves a painless death, unlike God," said Mr. Future to the security officers.

"What do you prefer? A bullet in the head, having your head chopped off, being hanged by a rope?" Mr. Truth asked Mr. Marriage.

"Poison, sweet poison, please," said Mr. Marriage.

"Do I have your permission for that? Are you okay with this request?" Mr. Truth asked the judges.

"Yes, please," said Child.

"Hold on," said Mrs. Woman. "He can have a sweet death, but we have suffered so much because of him. We need to kill his body, but I want to play with the colors of his blood."

"Of course you should, and you will, and I am sorry for what I have done to you. I wish you well," said Mr. Marriage, looking at Mrs. Woman and smiling.

Mr. Philosopher wrote about Mrs. Woman's request:

I want to taste his blood:

Let my pain smile by drinking his blood,

Let his blood make my lips smile again,

Let my wounded skin blossom again by soaking in his blood,

Let me comfort my tears by mixing his blood into them.

I want his blood. I want it bad.

Security brought a glass of whisky that was mixed with poison. Mr. Marriage grabbed the glass and was about to gulp it, when he stopped. "No, something is wrong. Not this way. I am not fucking dying this way. I have a last wish. Yes, I do have one."

The Assembly murmured in surprise, eager to hear Mr. Marriage's last wish.

Mr. Marriage continued, "When I look back at my life, I remember my shiny suit with the wealth of the past that followed my deals with God and JC. I see myself in white robes in the church, entertained by vows and other stories. Then, in the present, I see my modern day habits and smile. I know that I have made mistakes, but I have always looked to the future with hope. Not any more. I don't wish to. I don't care that my life is over. But one thing I regret is that I am dying before God. If I may, I request that you kill this bastard before me. This is my last wish: kill God before you kill me."

"I think that is fair," said Child.

God looked different with no facial hair and a shaved head. For the first time, people could see His real face. His facial hair had always obscured most of His eyes, mouth, and face, but now the green reptilian eyes and patchy red skin were clearly visible, and the snarky grin fixed on His face barely concealed His protruding canines, all of which was unsettling for the people in the gallery

Security made God stand. But they refused to hang Him. They were afraid to do so.

"Who will hang God? It won't be easy, and every man is afraid to kill Him," said Mr. Truth.

"I will kill him," said Child. "And I will not do it by hanging; I will do it with my stupid pocketknife."

Child stepped down from the judges' box, and walked towards God with its little blunt knife in its hand. It looked into God's eyes and slowly freed God's white robes from His body. It took *The H Book* from God's pocket and ordered the others to burn it. God could do nothing but watch helplessly as the book turned to ash. Tears ran down His cheeks.

Next, Child slowly ran its finger down God's chest, as if its fingers were writing something. Child was making the symbol of a cross on God's chest. It took its knife and, moving slowly, cut open the skin on God's chest to see if God could bleed. To its surprise, God did bleed. Child skillfully used the knife and cut the cross sign deeper into His chest and stomach. As the blood left His body, God began to die a slow and agonizing death.

"Any last wishes, God?" asked Child earnestly, removing the shoe from God's mouth.

"Yes, I do have one," said God.

Child touched God's blood with its thumb, smelled it, and

licked it to see if it was any different than human blood. It then pressed the cut on God's chest with its finger to feel His flesh.

"Go ahead and tell me, God. I think I know what you are going to ask," Child said.

"I cannot take the pain any more. Can you give me poison, please? I am afraid of the pain!" screamed God.

"I cannot," said Child. "I thought you would ask us to let you lead a prayer as your last wish. I am sorry, I cannot offer you an easy death."

Instead of screaming out loud, God whispered in Child's ear, "You know what, I hate you all. You are fucking jokers who just amuse Me with your obedience. There is nothing to be inspired by in you. You, kid, will one day become an adult and will follow some other god. You humans are made to be believers and followers. I hate you, kid."

Then He turned to the Assembly with hope in His eyes. God wanted to sign off on a good note, so that humans would remember Him as a forgiving God, but more, He still hoped that the men in the crowd would save him from Child.

God began weeping and said, "I still forgive everyone. I forgive even this innocent Child, though it is executing Me. In the name of the Father, I love you all, from the deepest corners of My heart."

Then God lurched forward, kissed Child on the mouth, and licked Child from chin to nose. He whispered, "This is how I kissed my Father before I killed Him," and winked.

Child took the knife and cut out God's tongue quickly. Blood shot onto Child's face.

"He cannot fool us any more with his sweet talk," shouted

Child. "You can string him up across the arch at the entrance of the Assembly, right where it is written: *The New Home of God,*" ordered Child.

"We still cannot believe that you are killing our dear lord God," said Mr. Man.

"Yes, I am, and it is indeed a pleasure to do so," said Child, walking back to its seat while wiping the blood off of its face.

"It is necessary, dude. No hard feelings, nothing personal," said Mr. Future to Mr. Man.

The blood started falling from God's body onto the ground. Security dragged His body off the stage. He was losing blood and consciousness. Security took His body and hung it upside down from the arch. Mr. Philosopher looked at the body and sang:

"Every person takes the name of God when he dies.

Now, it is the turn of our holy lord to cry and die.

Will he pray and if so, to whom?

Maybe he will say something new and due.

He has the same blood as you do.

He's made of the same mud as we knew.

He is dying to add to human achievement.

You are your king and remember nothing ancient.

Let his blood bring you reason and spring a new season."

From where they sat in the gallery, the humans were horrified by the naked body of God hanging and dripping blood from the majestic sand-colored arch. A few people began to cry. Most of them stared in shock. This was the end of the almighty and loving God.

MARRIAGELESS

Everyone stood silently and waited to see if the Earth would burst into a thousand pieces, if rains would start, if volcanoes would erupt, if floods would begin.

God died silently.

Nothing happened.

The people sighed in relief.

"Now, it's your turn, Mr. Marriage," said Child.

"Indeed, smart kid. I am tired of my own life, and more confused than ever. I thank you, kiddo," said Mr. Marriage, as he drank to his death, gulping the poisoned whisky.

"Mrs. Woman, he's all yours. You said you would feel better if you could play with Mr. Marriage's blood? Go ahead, you have our permission," said Child to Mrs. Woman.

Mrs. Woman fell to her knees, and paused as Mr. Marriage let out a last breath and died. A tear fell from her eye and slowly crawled down her cheek, though she was smiling. She remembered the physical and mental torture she had endured in the name of marriage. She remembered bleeding from the wounds made by Mr. Marriage. She thought back on the times she had been beaten, raped, and tortured for disobedience.

In her mind's eye, she could see her naked body on a stake, reaching to the moon. She could see men using her dead body for amusement. She saw Mr. Marriage laughing and encouraging the men.

Mrs. Woman came to her senses, remembered her oath, and jumped on him, scratching hysterically, her fingernails tearing open the already wounded skin of his face. She smeared some of Mr. Marriage's blood in her hair. Laughing feverishly, she washed

247

her face with Mr. Marriage's blood, attaining some peace with herself and their violent, abusive past.

"It's my time too," said Old Man. "There is no role for me to play in the absence of God, because I am exactly the opposite of God. Hence, I volunteer to leave humanity, and wish you all the best. On this day, the purpose of the AntiGodists has been achieved. I will fly away."

Suddenly, Old Man turned into a black angel with wide wings and the face of an ancient serpent, and flew around God and away into the sky, on his way to nowhere. Right before leaving everyone's view, the ancient serpent swooped down again, now carrying a bottomless pit on a chain around his neck. With his fangs, the angelic serpent grabbed God's body, which was tiny compared to the giant serpent. The serpent shoved God's body into the pit, and flew away into the unknown universe, disappearing from the Assembly.

Meanwhile, the security forces took Mr. Past to the forest and left him in the darkest part, so that he would never get back to human society. He would die alone.

Mr. Marriage's corpse was taken off the stage, and Mr. Truth asked the judges to come with him to witness his burial.

When the stage was empty, the people started moving out of the Assembly. Some walked with their heads down, thinking; some smiled to themselves. No one spoke. They were all thinking like individuals. They were not burdened by marriage or religion. They walked out of the Assembly, each one alone, and entered the future of a Marriageless and Godless society.

THE BURIAL

They buried Mr. Marriage outside the city, in the wide-open space near the grave of Mr. Rational. Everyone was silent for a few minutes, thinking about how different the world would be now.

A part of Mr. Man was worried about the future, and a part of him was free. He took Mrs. Woman's hands and told her, "I am sorry."

"For what? Don't we all have to promise to forget everything and walk from here with no memory of the past? I don't know what you are sorry for," said Mrs. Woman, and smiled.

Mr. Present was happy. He looked forward to presiding over the new Godless and Marriageless society until he grew old and passed the rule to Mr. Future.

Child was smiling at everyone. It knew it would grow up to be a free adult.

After the execution of Mr. Marriage and God, humans were on a path towards accepting everyone, as there was nothing to differentiate each person from the other. Faith did not exist, religion did not exist, and therefore, there was no good reason to kill each other.

With the death of Mr. Marriage, people would be open to sharing love and being loved by everyone they met throughout their lives. The old ideas of souls and soul mates were dead; the new idea was to share love with many people until one's journey on Earth came to an end.

The concept of marriage, which limited love to family and to one particular person, would never be heard of again. If an individual loved and stayed with only one other person for his or her entire life, this would happen because of love, not because of religion or marriage. The concepts of a primary partner, a secondary partner, and casual partners would all be commonplace. Children would be loved, but there would be no law dictating that one must marry and have children. And sex would not be an obligation; it would happen because of love and passion.

MARRIAGELESS

Mr. Philosopher looked at the grave of his friend, Mr. Rational, and said, "My friend, you have finally gotten your answers. You were right, we don't need Mr. Marriage any more."

History need not always inspire good; it can inspire evil, as well. Mr. Philosopher knew this, and he wrote a final poem in his book:

Dear lazy reader, you made it 'til the end;

Remember to start all over, and think again, my friend.

Question everything you were, all the time you've spent.

I apologize, but death was required.

I hope I've inspired before I now retire.

Characters die and rise, smile once before we all say our goodbyes.

Mr. Philosopher closed the book and smiled. His book, *MarriageLess*, was complete. He smiled again, satisfied.

"Can I take a look at it?" asked Mr. Man.

"Of course, why would he not show you?" said Mr. Truth. "In the end, it must be made available to everyone. I am sure he wrote it skillfully and philosophically."

"No, it's not written for everyone. It is written only for one person, and completing this book is important to me because of him," said Mr. Philosopher. As he capped his fountain pen and secured it in his pocket, Mr. Philosopher kissed the book and its yellow cover, and began tearing the book into pieces.

"I need to bury it with my dear friend, Mr. Rational. It was written in his memory," said Mr. Philosopher, smiling.

"But future generations might want to know about Mr. Marriage, who once lived. They will want to know about the Assembly. They will want to know about the historic decision that happened today," said Mr. Truth.

"For what?" asked Mr. Philosopher. "They should not know about Mr. Marriage at all; that's the way to have a new start."

He scattered the pieces of the book on Mr. Rational's grave and poured Mr. Rational's favorite whisky over them. He took a shot of the liquid, and then set fire to the pages. He watched the words and meanings and poems of *MarriageLess* rise above, fly off into nothing, and disappear.

Made in the USA
Charleston, SC
11 February 2017